Faith in My Hustla

T'yanna Sha-Nay

Text **Treasured** to **22828**
To subscribe to our Mailing List.
Interested in becoming a part of
the Treasured Publications
family?

Submit manuscripts to
Info@Treasuredpub.com

Faith in my Hustla

Acknowledgements

First and foremost, I would like to give thanks to the
Almighty for blessing me and keeping me highly favored.
There were so many times when giving up became my first
option and prayer my last. I'm better now and I understand
the power of prayer. Thank You, everything is possible with
You.

To my mother and father: there isn't much more a girl could
ask for than two loving and supportive parents. I love you
both dearly and appreciate the endless support and faith
you both have in me. Mommy, you always told me to
"write" and look at me now, beautiful. Dad, no matter what
I've done right or wrong you've been in my corner whether
near or far.

To my sisters: thank you for believing in me and being my
rule book for life, lol. Everything I am today you both have
played a major part in it. Tuniqua and Tierra, thank you
both. I love you to the moon and back and to the moon and
back again. Ty my sister/cousin: this wasn't only my dream
but yours as well and all your impromptu stories and the
endless amount of books we have read contributed to this

very moment. I love you so much, girlllllll. Yanna, Emmy, Iman, I love you all.

Tasha and Tish, thank you for being there, even when y'all weren't there, y'all were there. I look up to you both and love y'all more than anything. I know y'all want nothing but the best for me.

Sadie, Bria, and Kendearia, you three are the epitome of friendship and nothing short of family. The three of you, more so Sharoyale and Kendearia, have listened to me talk about writing a book since I was eighteen years old and now at twenty-two, it's finally more than just a dream of mine. Bria, thank you for all your crazy ideas and I'm glad this is something we all can enjoy.

Baby Jai and Kiana, there aren't enough words that can help me express how thankful I am for the both of you. All the talks we've shared helped me in more ways than one and I am overly appreciative of you both.

BEST, many don't see our vison but soon they will understand everything we have sacrificed and continue to sacrifice to be GREAT! I couldn't have a better best friend than you. I love you, best, thank you for always pushing me and believing in my dream.

There isn't a better group of girls that I'd want to go through all that we've went through together. From the fights to the laughs, you all have showed me nothing but a great deal of support from day one. Nine years of friendship is sometimes unheard of with eight females that are all so different, yet alike, in so many ways. We've beat the odds and did numbers from high school to college; we still made sure to put our friendship first. There was a time when I used to be so nervous to let y'all read my shizz, now I'm getting threatened for not finishing what I started. *Honor Thy Sister* was our baby as a group and trust I'll get it done.

Shanice and Shereece, I'm a better friend because of you both and a more conscious writer with the endless feedback you both give (Shan-nice). Danielle, Danielle, Danielle even when I took my writing as a joke you were smart enough to know that was just me hiding behind my fear of failing. Thank you for everything, baby. Na'Bintou "Noah" "my baby mama harder than a lot of you niggas", you've always saw something in me that I didn't see in myself because I was too caught up in everything and everyone else. I just want to thank you all for the motivation you all have given me to keep going. I love you all.

Carlnika, baby girl, thank you for believing in me and supporting me. I love you so much.

Equan, my brother, thank you for always believing in me, you're the best brother a girl could ask for. I appreciate the support you have shown me over the years.

Jason "Tyquan Simms", thank you for believing in me, kid! BK, since a kid you've always shown love and supported me even when I was too scared to come to practice and play ball, lol. I appreciate you.

Precious, sis, thank you!

Merlin, Elijah, Dymere, A.J, and Carl you guys are truly the best and we may not speak every day like we used to but I couldn't forget the love and support you all have showed me over the years. I love you all.

G/M, I could never forget all of our talks and the books we have shared. I love you so much, woman, thank you for everything! Always listening and always supporting.

Ms. Moore, thank you for being one of the ones to put a book in my hand and opening the doors of literature for me. You are truly appreciated.

Paris, Paris, Paris, you are nothing short than crazy but who am I to judge, sis, lol. Thank you for taking the time and wanting to see me succeed, they need more people like you in the world.

Quelly, you've always reached out and asked to read some of my work. Thank you, cousin, I love you.

Siara, sister, thank you for taking the time to always read my work from the beginning when I was just writing because I knew how. I appreciate all the support, sis!

Treasureeeeeeeeeeee! Man, listen, without you this would all still be a dream to me and I'd still be revising the same book I wrote in 2013. You are more than a publisher but an amazing individual and FRIEND! You know I don't even play with you, sis, so again thank you for everything! You are truly the best, QUEEN.

If you feel I forgot you or left something out, blame it on my mind and not my heart. Thank you to EVERYONE who offered an encouraging word or took the time out to understand what I was doing and why. If I could list you all I would. Oh, and to those who didn't, YOU DO NOT MATTER, BOO!

To my family, I love you all, thank you for everything!

This book is dedicated to Kahdijah M. Boben. My SISTER and FRIEND, I love you so much.

Synopsis:

How far would you go in the name of love? How much are you willing to sacrifice for the one you love? For Erin Singleton, there was no limit to her love. Genuine love is all she knows. Coming up in a two-parent household, surrounded by a loving family was all she had known. That is until the pressure of being a Singleton becomes too much and she leaves the safety net of her parents' home for the unknown. Faced with uncertainty and life changing decisions to make, Erin sets out to make it on her own until she meets him.

Kymani Martin made it easy for Erin to fall for him. He was the listening ear when she needed it and also a protector. He didn't have much either, but what drew Erin to him was his ambition. It was street ambition, but ambition none the less. Coming from an upbringing much different from Erin's, Kymani had been alone long before she had arrived. In a city with no family, all he knew was how to survive. While Erin ran from the pain, Kymani ran towards it.

With his right hand, Tevin at his side. Kymani sets out to conquer the streets and everything that's associated with them. While love wasn't on his to have list, he welcomed it when it came to Erin because she was down for him and supported his come up.

They say it's good to stay down until you come up. But will that ring true for Erin? Will the sacrifice she makes in the name of her relationship be worth it, or will she find out just how bad things can get when you put all your faith in a hustla?

Prologue

Erin

Late at night when all the world is sleeping... I'd like to say that I stay up and think about the love of my life. Usually I do. But tonight, was different. I missed him. Even though he was lying right next to me, I was longing for him. For the past two years, Kymani had been everything I needed. A lot of people would have never understood the decisions I made or even tried to. They would never see the silver lining in me leaving a place where I was afforded the luxury of having everything my heart desired to a life where I didn't know where my next meal was going to come from. At least until I met Kymani. He didn't have much of anything to offer me, but he offered himself. He offered understanding, compassion, companionship, and a promise that things would work out for us in the end. He's stuck by that, and for the most part, the stars were aligning and things were working in our favor. That's why I missed him. That's why I was longing for him.

"Baby E, go to sleep," Kymani groaned while reaching his arm over to where I sat with my back pressed against the headboard.

"Can't sleep," I sighed while moving closer to him so he could wrap his arm around my mid-section.

"Damn, the dick wasn't enough to put you in a coma tonight."

I chuckled. "It was." I couldn't remember a time where Kymani and I had sex and I didn't want to pass out right after. I'm surprised he was even up for it. After a week away from home on the road, he came home with one thing on his mind.

"Nah, we gotta go another round." He pulled me down towards him and pressed his lips against mine.

"I love you," I spoke through heavy breaths.

"I love you too, E. You good?" he questioned. Kymani could always sense when something was off with me.

Normally, I would tell him he was right, but tonight I had to lie. "I'm good."

Didn't want to ruin our…

Bang, bang, bang

Loud bangs could be heard coming from the front of the apartment, alarming Kymani and me. Well him. I sighed, already knowing what was next.

"Fuck is banging on the door this late? Prolly that nigga, Tevin. My phone dead and shit he probably was calling me. I swear his ass can't function without me," Kymani griped as he slowly climbed out of bed and grabbed the Nike shorts that were on the foot of the bed on my side.

He took a few steps towards the bedroom door and opened it. With each step he took, I sighed a little, awaiting the inevitable.

Bang, bang, bang

The thuds against the door were even clearer.

"FBI, open up!"

"The feds?" Kymani turned toward me with a pained expression on his face.

Panic set in as he backed away from the bedroom door.

"This shit can't be happening right now," he barked while making his way over to the closet.

I watched him rummage through it for a few seconds before calling after him.

"Kymani. Ky! Kymani!"

"What!" I know he didn't mean to yell at me the way he did, but it didn't stop me from jumping. "Where all my shit, E? Why you sitting there all calm like all my work and pieces not in this crib with us?"

My heart broke as I pulled myself out of the bed.

"Don't worry about that. I took care of everything."

"E, what are you talking about, man?"

"I love you, Kymani. Everything you've done for me? For us? It can't end now. We've come too far. You've worked too hard."

Grabbing Kymani's sweats that I had on when he came home, I slipped back into them and tossed my hair in a messy ponytail using the scrunchie that was on my wrist.

"Which is why I'm trying to get the work out of here before they come in. They not going to knock for much longer."

"Stop worrying about that and listen to me. You love me, right?"

"You know I do." He assured me. Even though he didn't have to tell me because it showed in the way he spoke to me, as well as how he treated me, his mannerisms toward me told me all I needed to know.

Finally, after slipping on a t-shirt, I made my way over to where he stood. I wrapped my arms around him and pulled him into me.

"Finish what we started and continue holding me down."

"There will never be a time that I don't hold you down, Erin. But between you and the boys at my door, I'm fucked up right now."

Pushing my five-foot-five-inch frame onto my tippy toes, I gently placed my lips against his and inhaled his scent. A scent that I would always love because it belonged to him. A lone tear cascaded down my cheek and the agonizing feeling in the pit of my stomach intensified. This was it.

"I love you," I spoke through our kiss.

I backed away from him before I broke down. Before he could respond, I turned my back toward him and headed toward the front door.

"I'm coming," I called out so that they would stop banging.

I reached the door, unlocked it, and before pulling it open, I glanced back to find Kymani standing there confused.

"Everything we dreamed and spoke about, make it happen," I instructed him while opening the door.

"Erin Singleton?"

I nodded, turned around, and put my arms behind my back.

"Erin Singleton, you have the right to remain silent anything you say can and will be…"

I drowned the agent out. That wasn't the last thing I wanted to hear.

"What the fuck is going on?" Kymani barked before rushing over to us.

"Kymani, stop!" I screamed, halting his steps. "I love you."

"E. What the fuck, man. I love you, why…"

Chapter One

Five years later…

Kymani

"Daddy, daddy!" Azia squealed before running in my direction and leaping into my arms. My baby girl was five going on forty, if it wasn't for her long-beaded braids and small voice sometimes I felt like I was talking to her mom. I watched as my daughter swung her hair with every step she took, the beads at the end of her braids caused her to be extra.

"Hey, Princess." Azia leapt into my waiting arms and I spun her around. I couldn't hold back the smile that spread across my face as she blessed me with a million kisses. Her bright, brown eyes resembled mine and looking at her I saw that my genes were strong. Azia was my twin and I couldn't deny her if I wanted to.

"Daddy, stop, I dizzy." Her laugh was infectious and so was her smile. I knew if there was one thing I was good at other than being a hustla, it was making beautiful babies. Azia was my everything and I thanked God every morning for blessing me with such a smart and beautiful baby girl.

"Kymani, put her down before you get her worked up. I'm not about to chase her around this mall," Lia whined as I continued to toss Azia around in the air.

"Mommy, never lets us have our fun right, Princess?" Azia was too busy laughing to answer me, so she just shook her head yes. Lia was such a worry wart that with every move Azia and I made she was either telling us to be careful or slow down.

"So, what you trying to get, Ma? I'm not trying to be in the mall all day.

"I just have to get Azia something for picture day. My mom wants us all to take pictures so she can replace the old ones hanging in the house." I had so much stuff to do today and playing in the mall with Lia wasn't in my plans, but when she woke me up complaining that Azia had nothing to wear for her family's annual picture day, I knew there was no telling her ass no. No was a word she'd never heard and I didn't make it any better because I spoiled her and Azia rotten. There wasn't anything that their hearts desired that they didn't have, especially Azia.

I was the happiest man alive when they opened Lia and Azia's favorite store, Justice at Green Acres Mall, as much money I spent in here I should've became part owner or some shit. I couldn't front, though, this little store had everything Azia loved, so it saved me a lot of time when I had to shop for her. In the beginning, you couldn't catch me doing shit like this because I was so detached from what it meant to be a father. I didn't have my father in my life, so to me being a good father was making sure that they wanted for nothing; not going on dates to the mall or the movies, none of that shit, but after a year Lia got my ass in shape quick.

"Daddy, eat, eat." Azia was in my arms talking my head off as we made our way back to the car. She had just eaten a pretzel from Auntie Annie's, so I wasn't sure how she was hungry right now, but what baby girl wants she gets.

"What you wanna eat, A?" I looked down at my Apple watch to check the time and it was going on one o'clock, and I had a lot of running around to do before I picked Erin up tomorrow.

Since Erin got knocked I'd been on grind mode building our empire just how we planned five years ago. Tevin had been holding it down since a nigga had next to nothing, so it was only right I brought my right-hand man to the top with me. Tevin and Erin were the only two people I trusted, and time and time again I found myself going out my way for niggas who meant me no good. If E was here, she would have definitely got in my ass for it. I'd been trying to distance myself from the bullshit for the past month so that she came home to no drama.

"Aye, Lia, I'm going to drop y'all at the crib. I have some shit I need to handle." I didn't even have to look her way to know that she was grilling my ass, but the shit I had to do couldn't be put off for anyone, not even her. I ignored her as she sucked her teeth and strapped baby girl in her car seat.

"Stuff like what, Mani? What could possibly be more important than me and Azia?"

"You know there isn't anything more important than my daughter. She straight tho, so all that shit you talking is irrelevant." I turned the music up and listened to the same three songs over and over. I swear I hated the radio, but I knew if I hooked my phone up Lia would have taken that as an open opportunity to go through my shit, and I didn't have time for her bullshit today. Today was intended to be a good day, one of the happiest days in five years for me, aside from the day Azia was born. I missed the hell out of Erin and those little three second visits did nothing for a nigga like me. I needed her in the worst way. I missed her smile and goofy laugh; I missed the way she took care of a nigga and always put my needs over hers. Erin was my everything.

"Mani, slow down, you're speeding." I ignored Lia's whining ass and looked through the rearview mirror to check on Azia and like always she was knocked. I was only going a little over the speed limit; Lia just wanted to be Lia.

"I'm going to call you. Make sure you feed my kid and redo her braids before y'all take pictures tomorrow."

"Why are you dropping us off here? Why can't we go back to your house?"

"Lia, you cried and begged for this spot. Now you tripping when I bring you home to YOUR house. I have to go, man." Shit between Lia wasn't even supposed to go this far, but it just happened and next thing I knew I had two people calling me daddy. At first I was sick, but Lia grew on me, and because she was keen to the street shit I was into it made it that much easier for me to get comfortable with her ass. When I was with her, I wasn't Ky or Money, I was regular ass Kymani Martin that saved up his checks from working and started my own Car Wash in Queens.

"So, you're going to miss picture day, too, I guess?" I took pictures with my daughter on the regular, and I didn't really rock with Lia's peoples that heavy, so whether I had shit to do or not, I wasn't making picture day anyway and she knew that shit. Azia was still knocked out so I waited until Lia was safely inside the house before I pulled off, breaking almost every rule they enforced when I went for my L's.

***

I watched as she stood there, looking around with a sad expression on her face, and I smiled inside because, even after five years in the pen, Erin was the baddest female I've ever laid eyes on. I'm guessing because of the car I was in she didn't notice me sitting right in front of her. The way she stood there staring off into space as if her mind was working overtime trying to figure out where the fuck I was at brought me back to the time we first met.

E was fifteen and I was a little nigga still trying to find his way and it had to be God that brought us together because I had no business on Farmers and 147th, but a nigga was hungry and McDonald's was the closest thing to me at the time and I hardly ate there. It was raining something crazy and I was kicking myself in the ass for even coming all the way over here for a weak ass meal, but all that changed when I pulled off and saw this girl standing in the rain on 175th near the shelter.

"Hey, ma, you need an umbrella?" I called out to her from the comfort of my front seat of my beat-up Camry. My shit wasn't all that, but it got me from point A to point B just fine. She was standing there soaked. When she didn't answer me, I grabbed the umbrella and made my way over to where she was standing.

"I have an umbrella if you want it." Again nothing, she just stood there lost in her thoughts.

"Can I help you?" she nastily asked me as she looked me up and down.

"Nah, ma, I'm trying to help you. It's raining and you out here getting soaked and shit. I have an extra umbrella is what I was trying to tell you."

"Nah, pa, I'm good. Thanks. I don't need shit from some stranger." I wanted to say more, but it was raining and her ass was being rude just because, so I tucked the umbrella under her arm against her will and turned en-route back to my car.

"Why me? I'm only fifteen; what am I supposed to do? If I go in this shelter, then the life I once knew is over for good and there is no going back. Why the fuck is it a problem that I want to be my own person?" I stopped midstride and turned to see shawty yelling and screaming at the air.

"Chill, ma, slow down. Look it's raining; let me get you something to eat and out this rain and you can tell me all about your fucked-up ass life." I chuckled and surprisingly she smiled. It was a weak smile, but it was progress. I knew I was going to have my hands full with her because it took me to say some slick shit to get her to smile.

"Hey, ma, you need an umbrella?" It wasn't raining, but I knew once she heard my voice she'd know it was me.

"Kyyyyyyyyy," Erin squealed as I emerged from the car. The shimmer behind her eyes was still there; I was glad she didn't lose sight of herself in that fucked up institution.

"Erinnnnnnnnnn." I mocked her as I pulled her in for a hug and lifted her off her feet and showered her face with kisses, just like Azia had did me earlier. I waited for years to hold her in my arms without some fat ass guard breathing down our back every time we stared at each other too long on our visits.

"You're late," she whined in between my kisses. I didn't want to let her go. I dreamed of this moment on the regular, and it felt like at any moment Lia was about to start yelling that it was time for me to wake up or Azia was going to start jumping on me while I tried to sleep.

"Baby, I've been here. You just ain't expect a nigga to pull up in this boss ass ride." I kept Erin in my arms as I walked her over to the all-black 2017 BMW x5. I was never into flashy ass cars, so I knew Erin was expecting me to pull up in some regular degular shit. After today though, all this shit was hers. I waited five whole years to spoil her little ass rotten, and I finally had the opportunity to do so.

"I missed you so much, stink." I knew today was emotional for her, but I didn't expect my ride or die to start that crying shit. As much as she tried to muffle her groans and hide her tears as she buried her face in the crook of my neck, I knew. We were one; I knew everything about Erin Singleton.

"Don't cry, baby. I have a surprise for you, and, if you cry now, you're not going to have any tears left for my popping ass surprise." I placed Erin in the passenger seat and kissed her lips one more time before I walked over to the driver's side.

When I found out Erin was being released a few months back, I hired the best contractors to renovate this big ass house I had built from the ground up awhile back that was ducked off in Queens. The seven bedrooms and six-bathroom, two story family brick home was a place I wanted E to be able to call home so that her five years sitting up became a distant memory. I wanted her to be able to have more than enough room to move around freely and sleep in a different room every day of the week if she wanted. Erin loved movies so I made sure they took their time with her theater room since that would be a place she spent most of her time. She could sit in that room for the rest of her life if she wanted. She was forever good and that was on my granny.

"Ky, whose big ass house is this?" We had just pulled up to the house and I had to shake her to get her up. The smooth sounds of my boy, Trigga Trey, still put her ass to sleep. Whenever I wanted Erin to take her ass to bed and sit down somewhere, I would give her some dick and put Trigga on and her ass would be sound asleep in minutes.

"Yours, E, this is all yours. The house, this car, the three cars in the garage, all yours, beloved. I wanted to give you the world, but they wouldn't let a nigga buy it. Something about democracy imbalance or some shit."

"You're a whole fool. I don't know what to say."

"Don't say shit; get to crying. Show a nigga you appreciate him. I told your ass to stop all that cryin' earlier and save them tears for this very moment."

"Fuck you. I wanna see inside; come on." She grabbed my hand and I allowed her to lead the way inside her new home as I tossed her the keys. I would have my man, Jimmy, come through tomorrow to hook up her security system to her liking. E went straight for the stairs and I was glad because she was saving the best for last. As we went through the five rooms that were on the second floor, she admired the calm decorum and pointed out a few things she wanted to change. I wasn't tripping; this was her world, I was just living in it.

"Kymani Naim Martin, you didn't"

"Erin Cy'mone Singleton Martin, I did." She side-eyed me when I added my last name like she always did, but the tears that were now flowing freely down her beautiful face gave me all the confirmation I needed. I knew the movie room would be the room she loved the most and the nigga, Tevin, clowned me for it, but I knew Erin she was tough on the outside and sweet as candy on the inside. I had them blow up posters of her favorite movies from *The Wood*, *Paid in Full*, *Biker Boyz*, *The Blind Side*, and her all-time favorite, *Love & Basketball*. I even had the movie tickets she would save in our top draw framed and scattered throughout the room.

"Ky, I love it. Thank you so much. Oh, my goshhhhhhh; I love this sooo much." Her tear stained face damped my sweatshirt a little and I didn't mind one bit. The rest of the night, after she showered and changed into something more suitable for the occasion, we put a dent in all the movies she missed out on while she was gone. I had her closet stocked from her favorite sneakers to shoes along with her favorite designers, which at the time were True Religion, Taverniti, Forever 21, Nudie Jeans, G-Star, H&M, Nike, Ralph Lauren, Adidas, Nautica, and all the other shit we wore back then. I also upgraded my baby girl to all the new shit people were so crazy over like Kenzo, Givenchy, Play Clothing, A Bathing Ape, Balmain, all that good shit. E was laced to the nines. She had enough shit in her closet that she didn't have to go shopping for another year and a half if she didn't want to. I would say two or three, but the way Erin shopped I knew that was farfetched.

"You really did it. Everything you said you would, Ky; you got it done. All our late-night talks and plans are really in the works, and I'm really proud of you. I never thought this far ahead when I walked out that door five years ago."

"E, you really think I'd let your time apart from me be in vain, ma. Nah, a nigga put in extra hours to ensure you came home and never had to work a day in your life if you ain't want to. All this shit is for you; everything I ever did was for you, for us, ma. When all the rest of these niggas was sleep and laid up in the comfort of their own homes, I was on the block getting to that bag, ma. Tevin's ass could barely keep up with me, these niggas were out here hustling for the newest fits and kicks and the flyest whips, but me, I was on some other shit, some real beast mode shit. It was everything, Erin, and it'll forever be that," I told her and lifted my shirt to show her the tattoo I had dedicated to her. It read *Everything Erin my heart of hearts* with two love birds enclosed in a heart. That was my first of many tattoos, now a nigga was tatted up like a subway station in Harlem back in the day.

Tevin and I worked our way from the bottom up. Nothing was ever handed to us; everything we got, we worked for. The night, E, did that shit I'm not even gon' lie, I was fucked up for a minute. I couldn't understand why she did what she did for the life of me. I was the nigga; I was the one that was supposed to take that charge and sit up, not her. After our first visit, Erin took the time to break down the method to her madness and I could better understand her reasoning, and I appreciated the hell out of her ass.

From that day on, I vowed to grind harder than I ever did. I didn't realize it until E got arrested, but the time we spent together she was grooming me into the boss nigga that I was today. She was always dropping jewels and making me pay extra attention to shit I would have carelessly looked over.

At the time, I was already making a little noise, but the week after E was sentenced my name was sure to ring bells in every borough. Everybody knew Tee and Money. Niggas feared me, and the women from Staten Island to Far Rockaway loved me and my boy. Play time was over and we were applying pressure to these niggas' necks, and nothing moved without my approval. CK watched Tevin and I catch wreck since we were little niggas, and when we started putting in overtime, he noticed that too. CK was that nigga everybody wanted to be; even females envied him, and it was just my luck he took a liking to a young nigga that ain't have shit but his pride, his mental, and the hunger to get to that bag. Money started coming in fast when CK started giving us more responsibilities, and I had to boss up in the process. Everything E preached to me over the years, I was taking heed to.

Erin made sure everything about me read boss. I dressed like a boss, talked like a boss, thought like a boss, and hell I bet if you ask any chick, I tasted like a boss too. Max B was really my idol and I wasn't even from Harlem. When CK decided it was time for him to step down, he handed everything over to me and leveled a nigga's life all the way up. I was the youngest in charge and Tee was my left-hand man. E would always be my right; distance wasn't shit to me.

"I ain't even expect you to make it this far, but wifey had faith in you. I thought after your shorty got knocked that you were done for, but you proved me wrong. I've taught you everything you need to know. Not that you needed much teaching, but now you're prepared to take over and create your own legacy."

"This shit is bigger than me, K. I owe all this shit to E, and the fact that you trust a nigga like me just makes me wanna go even harder. I ain't never have shit, and after my granny passed, a nigga felt like he ain't belong to anything or anyone. That's neither here nor there though; I'm ready to get to that bag."

"Another thing, when you take over I need you to pay attention to the niggas you keep next to you in your circle. The realest nigga on my team is that same fine ass woman I lay up next to at night. Keep your head held high, Money,

and your eyes and ears to the streets at all times. You hear me."

"I got you, CK. I don't trust these niggas because none of these niggas' hearts beat like mine," I replied.

"I knew from the moment I saw your young ass hanging around here with that fine ass sister, that you were gon' takeover one day. All this shit is yours, kid, make sure you take care of home first. All that street shit is just perks to life. Now get your ass up out my shit and go be great." He placed his big ass medallion necklace over my head and sent me on my way after I dapped him up.

That conversation with CK stayed on my mind every day; K was as real as they came. There wasn't another nigga I would have rather learned this shit from. Between him and E, they had a nigga feeling like Big Meech, Nino Brown, Frank Lucas, and Rich Porter all wrapped up into one nigga, me, Money. I was never a fan of the name *Money,* but CK gave me that name and it just stuck. Everybody knew Money and it was either they loved me or hated me; there was no in-between. The chain CK gave me was the only jewelry that adorned my neck.

I couldn't sleep because I still felt like I was dreaming, and I felt like if I laid down with her, when I woke up I'd be back at my house in my bed alone or with Lia and Azia next to me. I stayed up and watched her sleep and learned her breathing pattern all over again. When six o'clock rolled around and she began to stir in her sleep, I took that as my cue to get up and go handle my hygiene after I carried her to the master bedroom and laid her in her California king-sized bed. Her master bedroom was like the room we once shared at our apartment but ten times better.

I heard her footsteps as she approached the kitchen and turned to face her.

"Good morning, beautiful."

"I thought you left; why didn't you sleep."

"What you mean? How you know I ain't sleep."

"I know you, Ky. Your eyes spoke to me before you did."

"Come sit so I can feed my baby. I know that bullshit food ain't do you no justice, and you barely touched the food you ordered last night." I moved around the kitchen, putting a little bit of everything on her plate. I didn't know what to make when I walked in her kitchen this morning, so I made everything she liked from pancakes, waffles, toast, cheese grits, bacon, shrimp, and poured her a glass of apple juice. Erin hated orange juice or anything with citrus. She claimed it made her skin itch or some shit like that. Shrimp and grits was her favorite breakfast meal, so I made sure to put more of that on her plate than anything else.

"Uh uh, Ky, get that away from me. I don't eat swine." I watched as she turned her face up at the plate and held her hands up in attempt to keep me from placing the plate in front of her.

"Niggas go to jail and come home Muslim like it's nothing. I better not see your ass eat a Skittle, no Jiffy cornbread, Starburst, none of that shit, ma." She was crying laughing, but I was dead ass serious.

"Real funny, nigga. Can you just make me a plate and hold the bacon?" Out of all the things E could've did with her time, her ass done went and converted to the other side. I was about to pull her card though to see just how hip she was. CK and Alana were five percenters, so I knew a little bit about the culture.

"What's today's mathematics?" More or less, E was a five percenter like most people who went to jail and converted. Supreme mathematics in the teachings of the Nation of Gods and Earths is a system of understanding numbers alongside concepts. Today was October 17th so if her shit was on point she'd know that it was Knowledge,

God, & Perfection all being born to Knowledge, Build, or
Destroy. She slyly smiled and bussed that shit out.

"Knowledge, God, & Perfection all being born to
Knowledge, Build, or Destroy."

"Check you the fuck out, E; aiight, I respect your shit
for now. Slip up and I'm on your ass, ma."

"Shut up, Ky. I thought you were feeding me." I
stared at her while she pouted, admiring her beauty. My
heart was really home, in the flesh. No more visiting her in
that ugly ass uniform or watching her cry through the gate
as I walked out of the same place she wished she could be
free from. E stayed ten toes down, but she was human and
there were plenty of visits where she let her frustrations
out. I wanted this moment right here to last forever.

"Ky, come on; I'm hungry," she whined as I held a
shrimp on the fork and took my time feeding her. I wasn't
even hungry anymore; seeing her full and satisfied filled me
up. I ate good for five years; I just wanted to cater to her
every need and want.

"I love you, Kymani Naim Martin," Erin said in-
between kisses. I couldn't keep my hands off her, and now
that she was fed and rested, we were about to make up for
five long years of loss time.

"I love you more, Erin Cy'mone Singleton-Martin."
We both laughed as I carried her upstairs to her bedroom. E
was my best friend, lover, and everything in one. I loved
everything about her, and I was just about to show her how
much I appreciated her.

"KYMANI! OH, MY GOD!" E yelled as she finally noticed the
ring on her finger while she tried to cover her face while I
carried her up the stairs. I don't know how she's just now
noticing that big ass rock on her finger. I smiled down at her
once we reached the master bedroom and I laid her on the
bed.

"Ky, what's this?"

"A ring; what it look like?"

"Don't get cute; you know what I mean."

"You think I was going to let you come home and
have your fine ass walking around here without these thirsty
ass niggas knowing wassup, nah, ma. This is for you; it's my
way of showing you that this what we have ain't nothing to
play with. This ring symbolizes everything I see in our future,
love, marriage, kids, hella kids, and the two of us getting to
that bag just like before.

Faith in my Hustla

"Thank you, stink; this is beautiful." I never felt so sure about anything in my life the way I felt about E. I knew she was it for me; E made me the man I was today.

Chapter Two

Erin

This past week was one that I dreamed about for five whole years. This house was so big and I was just getting used to sleeping in and moving around freely. When Ky was here, my house felt like a home and I had him all to myself. No phones, no interruptions, no outside, just Ky and I. Waking up this morning without him in my bed mad me sad, but the idea of finally going outside allowed me to push my many thoughts of Kymani to the back of my head.

Today I was finally going to get this head done. The two braids I was rocking weren't giving me life, and I was ready to feel the old Erin. My home girl, Cyn, was the only person I could think of when it came time to do my hair. Cyn had done my hair since I was a teenager and she was the only person I trusted to slay this wild thing on my head. With my mother's Native American background and my father being mixed, my hair was wild and curly on any given day if I didn't take the time to tame it.

I was all into this new beginnings lifestyle Ky was preaching, so I was thinking about switching it up and getting an install instead of my regular wash and set with the rollers or wearing my hair in its natural curly state. I asked Ky to track Cyn down for me and when he told me that she had her own shop on Merrick called Eternity and was no longer doing hair out of her mother's living room, I was so happy for her. Cyn was the only other females besides CK's wife, Alana, that I trusted enough to make sure that Ky was good while I was gone. When my parents gave in and let me go to Jeff instead of the private school I was enrolled in since kindergarten, I met Cynthia Maleeka Cummings. Cyn and I were inseparable and she was my best friend. Every visit Kymani made, Cyn made sure to send her love and her letters always kept me in good spirits.

As I walked out the house and into the three-car garage, I weighed my options and decided to push the silver 2016 sports Camaro that had my initials engraved in the headrest. Ky really took his time when he picked out my cars, and I didn't know which one I liked more out of the four I had. The x5 was my baby because that was my dream ride since I was in middle school but the Camaro, Benz G-wagon, and the 2017 Honda Accord were all fire.

May the lord protect me as the world gets hectic
My voice projected my life reflected

Nicki Minaj's distinct voice filled up my car as I pulled out of the driveway and plugged Cyn's shop address into my GPS. Thank God for google maps because for the life of me I couldn't remember how to get to Merrick. Ky said it was going to take me a while to get used to being back in the mix, but I didn't expect to lose my sense of direction because I was born and raised in Queens. I guess five years in an institution facility would do that to you. I wasn't tripping though because the times Ky and I did go outside, he was teaching me how get around a little.

Damn I wanna run to you

Hold you and kiss you tell you how I miss you

Thought I would have a son for you

But now it's officially over and I can't let you go

But I gotta let you know all the shit I did make it feel like I'm dying real slow,

'cause no one understands me they don't know what to do when I'm hurt when I'm angry

You was my friend and my man and my daddy,

You was there when...

The irritating iPhone ringtone interrupted my jam session as I turned down Merrick and watched as Ky's picture popped up on the screen to my iPhone. I swear it was like everything was ten times bigger than when I was home because this 6s Plus was way too big, but Ky said I just had to have it.

I laughed aloud when I saw that he saved himself under Daddy. I slid my non-manicured finger across the screen and made a mental note to hit the nail salon before I went back in the house.

"Where the fuck you goin', ma?" he asked once he realized I was in the comfort of my car rather than the house where he left me last night.

"On my way to Cyn's shop. Wassup?"

"Nothing just checking in. You ain't text or call a nigga all morning."

"Aww you miss me, stink; I miss you more. Where's Tevin?" I asked as I heard unfamiliar voices in the background and saw a few familiar faces as I pulled into the parking spot in front of the shop. Ky was outside somewhere and I knew Tevin couldn't be far behind.

"Yo, Tee, the phone, my nigga."

"Who that? If it's Niecy, my ass ain't here." I heard Tevin yell before he grabbed the phone from Ky and placed his hand over the camera.

"Wow, Tevin, it's like that?" I faked like I was hurt.

"Oh shit, it's just E; nigga why you ain't just say that? You know a nigga been ducking Niecy ass for a month."

"Brother, you still messing with Shaniece's crazy ass. I thought you learned your lesson when she stabbed your ass."

"Damn a nigga can't even trust his best friend with his darkest secrets," Tevin joked, referring to Ky.

"He's my best friend, too. Anyway, why haven't you called me, Tee? I've been home for over a week and this is the first time I've spoken to you."

"Man, your ass is still spoiled as ever. Money told me to leave y'all be and I was just following orders.

"And since when did you follow orders?" I asked as he laughed.

"You right, sis. I'm gonna get up with you tho' this nigga over here ice grilling me and shit. Welcome home, E." Tevin passed Ky back the phone and his smile caused me to smile even harder.

"Tell Cyn I said 'was poppin'' and call me when you get finished. I love you, E."

"Okay. I love you, too, Kymani." I hung up and grabbed the royal blue MCM bag that set in the passenger seat and exited the car. It was a little chilly, so I grabbed my black leather jacket from my bag and threw it on. As I walked through the shop, I felt like everyone was staring at me, but when I turned to look back, they'd turn their heads. One thing being locked up did to me was make me paranoid as ever.

"Erin? Oh, my God, Erinnnnnnnnn. Bitch, when'd they let your ass out?" Cyn pulled me into a hug once she was sure that it was me. Cyn still looked the same; her ass was just way bigger than it was when we were seventeen.

"Hey, Cyn, I've been home for about a week. Thanks for always checking on me and sending messages through Ky; you don't know how much that shit meant to me."

"Bihh, please, you's a real bitch, and after everything you and Ky did for me it was only right I made sure you were straight whenever he stopped by." I didn't know what she was talking about.
"Everything like what?" I asked confused.
"Oh, he really didn't tell you, huh?" She let out a small laugh and smiled as she went on to tell me that Ky helped her get her shop open.

"So, I guess it's safe to call you, boss, right?"

"Hell no, this is all you, Cyn. I'm just glad we could help."

"This is all us. Now come and let me do something to that head of yours." Cyn pulled me to the back where the sinks were.

After Cyn washed my hair, she led me over to her chair that was in the front of the shop. As she blew my hair out, Cyn caught me up on the day to day of the shop. I didn't wanna be rude, so I let her tell me all she wanted, but I had no intentions on coming in here and taking over or whatever she thought because, from the looks of it, Cyn was doing just fine.

"I think I'm going to do something different, Cyn." I watched as she looked at me through the mirror. Everyone was used to Erin with the wash and set, but I was looking to switch it up.

"Like what, E? Don't tell me you want me to cut all this beautiful hair off because I won't."

"I'm not that bold, Cyn, I was thinking of getting an install; you know something long and maybe color the ends."

"Girl, you had me scared for a minute. I got you; I have some PB Luxury hair in the back and it's the best out right now. You really trying to step out, huh, sis." I sat back and waited for Cyn to return with the hair and once I settled on the length she braided my hair in cornrows, leaving enough out for my leave out. While Cyn did my hair, we made small talk about everything under the sun. I appreciated the fact that she didn't bring up me being locked up because that was something I didn't want to talk about. I was leaving all that behind me and was focusing on living my life as a free woman.

Once Cyn finished my hair about three hours later, I was exhausted from sitting down for so long. Cyn's shop had a nail bar connected to it and I was glad I didn't have to go far in search of someone to do my nails. I hadn't had my hair and nails done in five years and I forgot how good I looked when I was done up.

"Now that's the E I know." I heard Ky's voice as I was looking myself over in the full-length mirror that was in the back of the shop.

"Ky, what are you doing here?" I was surprised to see him because he didn't say that he was coming over here.

"I missed you, ma. I wanna be where you are, anywhere you are," he sang into my ear mimicking Michael Jackson. I grabbed the side of his face as he continued to sing in my ear and we just stood there in the mirror with our reflections staring back at us as Ky gave me a miniature concert in the back of Cyn's shop.

"Aww don't y'all look cute. I remember all the times Ky fell asleep on my mama's living room couch waiting for you to get your hair done," Cyn said, breaking us from our moment.

"Yeah, I used to hate that shit."

"Nobody forced you to stay, Ky. You was just scared E was gonna run into one of those buff ass Jamsey brothers that lived next door to Cyn's fine ass," Tevin said.

"Tevinnnnnnn. Hi, brother." I ran to him leaving Ky standing there.

"Wass good, E. A nigga happy they finally freed your ass. I was sick of my boy out here moping around and shit."

"Hello to you, too, Tevin."

"Wassup, Cynthia, how you?" Cyn rolled her eyes and ignored Tevin as we all made our way to Cyn's spacious office.

Since I was able to get my nails and hair done in the same establishment, I had time to spare. Not like I had plans to do anything else anyway. Sitting with Ky, Tevin, and Cyn brought back memories when we would all chill in Ky's and my apartment. The vibe I was getting from Tevin and Cyn was telling me that there was a lot that I missed out on. We all used to be super cool but whenever Tevin said anything I caught Cyn rolling her eyes or sucking her teeth. I wanted to ask, but I was going to wait until it was just me and Cyn in the room because Tevin was always extra.

"Yo, Tev, we got to bounce, bro. E, I'm going to call you aiigh, ma." I watched Ky as he stood and gave Cyn a hug before stopping in front of me. I hungrily watched as he adjusted himself and ran his hands over his deep waves as he stood in front of me. I pulled Ky down to me and kissed his juicy lips. Usually I hated public affection, but Kymani was looking very daddyish in his True Religion Jeans and black Crate sweater with his black and red retro twelves.

"Get a room."

"Come on, bro." Tevin pulled Ky away as I sat there savoring the taste of his lips.

"Y'all are just too cute, E. So, what are you trying to get into? Your hair is laid and you look good as fuck. You gotta step out and let everyone know the baddest bitch is back." Cyn was crazy, but stepping out didn't sound too bad. I had so much shit in my closet that I was excited to pick something out to wear.

"My homegirl, Naya, is having her birthday outing at Lituations tonight. I know your ass don't know what Lituations is, but it'll be fun, I promise." Cyn could have told me we were going to Applebee's and I still would have been excited. It was going on seven-thirty and I didn't even realize that we'd been back here that long. Cyn told one of her workers to lock up and we left to head to her house so that she could get her things. Cyn was probably the only friend I had, and I didn't mind bringing her back to my house. Hell, if she asked to move in I would let her ass because that house was just too big for me to be there all by myself. Kymani would be in and out the house as he pleased and that would leave me alone majority of the day with nothing to do. Cyn didn't know it yet, but I planned on holding her hostage.

Once we made it to my house, it was a little after eight-thirty, and Cyn said we weren't leaving until ten or eleven so I used the time to show Cyn around.

"Damn, E, Ky really set you up. That boy worships the ground you walk on and I think it's so cute. You are so lucky because Tevin's ass is another story." Boom, I knew it would come up sooner or later.

"Wassup with you and my brother? Y'all messed around or something?" We were in my living room and she had my full attention. It felt good to finally be able to sit and have girl talk rather than arguing and fighting with those irritating ass females I was locked up with.

"Messed around? Girl, Tevin and I were damn near living together, but he couldn't keep his dick in his pants and ended up sleeping with one of my client's home girls and the bitch couldn't wait to throw the shit in my face. I confronted his ass and he didn't even try to deny it. I couldn't keep getting my heart broken with Tevin so I knew it was best that I left him alone altogether. So I packed my shit and left, and that's when Ky came to me with the idea of opening up a shop to clean some of his money up and to give you something to do when you came home." I couldn't believe Tevin's ass, my sweet brother, wasn't so sweet anymore, and I swore there was something different about him, but I couldn't put my finger on it.

"It was like once CK gave Ky the green light something changed in Tevin. The sweet romantic dude I fell in love with just up and vanished as soon as the money started coming in consistently. That was over two years ago though, E. I'm over the shit now."

"I can't believe Kymani never mentioned that to me."

"Girl, you know Ky ain't into all that messy shit. Ain't nobody pressed over Tevin's ass, though. Let's go find you something to wear tonight; I saw all that shit in your closet. I don't even have to go to the mall anymore; I could just come take your shit."

After rummaging through my closet, I decided to wear my denim distressed jeans and a Kenzo t-shirt that I knew nothing about but the tiger was giving me life. I topped my outfit off with a nude pair of red bottoms. Cyn's outfit was similar to mine after she found her something new to wear in my closet.

"Okay, it's going on ten o'clock; we should shower and stuff."

"You could use the bathroom across the hall. There's fresh towels and wash cloths in there, too."

***

"Remember that night you snuck out the house to come with me to see Keith's fine ass on 125th."

"Yeah, bitch, and Kymani dragged my ass from his building all the way to the car. How could I forget? That was the first fight Ky and I ever had because your ass wanted to be hot in the pants."

48

"Bihh, you never told me no. You low-key wanted to go because Robert's fine ass was up there at the game." I damn near choked on my water when Cyn said that. Robert had the biggest crush on me back in the day and Kymani hated that man's guts with a passion. Just the mention of his name had me reminiscing to all the times Kymani wanted to beat my ass for being around Cyn when she hung with Robert and Keith.

This was a nice calm spot, but I just didn't expect it to be this small. With a name like Lituations, I figured we were about to walk into some big ass club, but this was more to my liking anyhow. After 1,825 days of being incarcerated, it felt good to be out and Cyn was making sure I had a good time. Her home girls were aiigh, but I wasn't in the business of making friends so I was chilling in the cut. There was a decent amount of people out tonight and the DJ was giving me life with his old-school playlist because I was so out the loop when it came to these new artists like Lil' Yachty and them other fools. The only new artist I was hip to was A-Boogie because they played his music upstate all day, every day.

Raindrops, drop tops (drop top)
Smokin' on cookie in the hotbox (cookie)

Fuckin' on your bitch she a thot, thot, thot (thot)

I rapped along to the song as Cyn stood a few feet

away from me, dancing. I was watching her like a hawk

because she'd been taking shots back like there was no

tomorrow.

"Sis, come dance with me. It's your first night out,

and you look good as fuck. There is no reason you should be

sitting here babysitting that damn water." Cyn pulled me to

my feet and over to the small open area where she was

previously dancing and we rapped along to the song

together while I tried my best to keep up with her. It had

been so long since I danced that I felt a little uncomfortable,

but Cyn was the perfect hype man and she had amped my

ass up good because all eyes were on us as we danced

together. I used to dance for Ky all the time in the house

since I wasn't able to attend all the hood parties and do

ratchet things with my friends like every other teenager I

knew. My parents used to have me on such a short leash

that every move I made there was someone watching me. I

was picked up and dropped off to school every day, leaving

me with no freedom at all. I hadn't thought about my

parents for five whole years, but here I was at a club for the

first time in my life finally being able to do 'ratchet things with my friend' and all I could think about was the life I had before all this, before Kymani.

"Don't look now, but I think my brother is stalking you," I whispered in Cyn's ear as I watched Tevin approach us with another dude I didn't know.

This was probably my first time in my whole life that I'd seen Tevin without Ky because when you saw one you almost always saw the other, especially if they were out and about. I watched as Cyn's whole demeanor changed as Tevin was in full eye view, and from the conversations we had I knew Cyn still had feelings for Tevin; she just didn't want to deal with all the drama that came with him.

"Sis, Mani know your ass out here with all these niggas?" I looked around making sure he was talking to me because maybe one of these other bitches was his sis and messed with a Mani because there wasn't even a nigga in sight where Cyn and I were. Kymani was right in the bed waiting on me to get home. He knew exactly where I was. Tevin was tripping because he never came at me like that before, and he had me fucked up because I felt a way about how he worded the shit that just came out his mouth.

"I'm grown don't play, Tevin. Does Mani know your ass is out here with random ass niggas, tho?" I questioned, gaining the attention of his friend.

Instead of responding to me, Tevin waved me off and approached a lustful Cyn. I could tell by the way he grabbed her up their conversation wasn't one I wanted to be around for, so while they engaged in what looked like a heated conversation I took that as my cue to sit down. There was an open seat at the bar, thank God, because the seating in here was very limited. I wanted to leave the owner a couple thousand to get some more chairs and knock down a wall or three. That's how small this place was; I was sure that their capacity limit was no more than 100 people, if that.

"So wassup, ma? Can I get your name?" I was sitting here, minding my own business and watching Cyn's home girl battle this dude. I don't know where Tevin found this nigga at, but I wished he would disappear. He couldn't have been around long if he didn't even know who I was or even had the balls to step to me knowing how Ky got down.

"Not interested," I simply said as I watched Tevin walk over to us with a scowl on his face. I kind of felt bad for him because I could see the chemistry him and Cyn had, and each time she was playing him to the left, but I was still in my feelings.

"He big mad or little mad, Cyn?" We both laughed as Tevin stood there looking all sad and shit. I was ready to go, though, before I hurt his homeboy's feelings for saying the wrong thing because he was too comfortable approaching me.

"You ready, E?" I was now standing with my Louis wallet in hand and I guess the irritation was written all over my face.

"Yeah, I'm hungry. I don't know where anything is anymore because the other day I thought I was going to IHOP and my ass got lost. I want some pancakes though."

"The diner is open; that's the best I could do for you, boo. Let me say bye to Naya and them and we could leave."

"Cyn, you heard what I said, ma; don't have a nigga waiting before I have to show my ass, aiigh."

"Not tonight, Tevin." We waited for Tevin and his lackey to dip before we hopped in my Camaro and were en-route to the diner. I wanted to stay and eat, but when Ky called my phone I just wanted to be up under him. Cyn knew she was going to meet up with Tevin because she kept bringing the shit up while we drove to get something to eat.

I was all for it, though, because I was in no position to put my two cents in on their situationship. Plus the way she spoke about him all day every day, I knew the love was still there.

Chapter Three

Kymani

Something told me to call before I came over here, but when I woke up to over fifty missed calls from Lia, and a few from her folks, I automatically thought something was wrong with Azia, so I did ninety over here, preparing myself for the worst, not this bullshit. Azia had really bad asthma episodes and had been having them for the past year, but about three months ago, the Dr. said she was doing way better. I had been in the house for a hot second and Lia was already on my ass about where I've been.

"A whole week, Kymani? Really? Your daughter has been asking for you every day. Where were you, Ky?"

"Lia, man, I told you I had some shit to handle and that I was going to be busy. If your ass would have answered my calls, instead of being petty, my daughter would have been able to speak to me and see me. Technology is a motherfucker if you ain't know." Lia side eyed me before she spoke again and I savored the moment her ass was quiet. All this crying and nagging shit wasn't her; well, at least it hadn't been

"I swear it's like you've been acting funny for the past few months, but I've been letting it slide. All the phone calls and being gone majority of the day. All of it I let slide, but now, Ky, I don't know." Lia was tripping as always and a nigga was over her complaining and whining. Her ass whined more than baby girl. If I would have known Azia wasn't even here, I would have never pulled up on Lia's ass.

"Aye, Li, I'm gon'; holla at you. Bring my fucking daughter home before you start blowing a nigga phone up and shit." Lia stood there, looking stupid. I grabbed my leather jacket off the couch and bounced. There was no need for me to stick around; I could have been laid up rubbings on E's phat ass, but instead I was here tending to Lia's cry baby ass.

Lately, I've been giving this nigga, PNB, a chance because he was all Erin talked about, and a few of the songs she played in the crib went hard. The loud I had rolled up was about to calm my nerves because Lia had me on ten with her irritating ass. Every time I got high, I contemplated selling the shit because everybody I knew got high, and if you had that fye then the shit would sell itself. Everybody smoked marijuana from grannies to high school kids.

My Heart: What time are you coming home? I wanna cook, but I don't wanna eat alone.

I had to go check on Tevin and make sure his ass wasn't bullshitting before I headed home to Erin. It was only going on four and I didn't plan on hitting the crib until like eleven, but since E texted me I was going to make sure I was in at a decent hour, even though I knew Cyn's ass was probably right there when she sent the text.

Me: Ma, a nigga don't have insurance, so don't burn nothing. I'll be home right after I check Tevin and them niggas.

My Heart: Whatever, nigga, don't forget who taught your peanut butter and jelly for breakfast, lunch, and dinner ass how to cook.

Me: Real funny, E. I bossed up though. Your ass ain't miss a meal yet thanks to me. I'll be home at a decent hour though. Tell Cyn's ass I said to go home lol.

My Heart: Ain't gonna happen. We'll see you when you get home. I love you, stink.

E wasn't playing when she said Cyn wasn't leaving because almost every other day Cynthia's ass was in our crib. I ain't complain because Cyn knew how to not overstay her welcome. She went home every night and didn't trip when I wanted E all to myself. I understood where my boy, Rock, was coming from when he said *I want you all to myself, I swear you don't need nobody else, I swear.* I was grateful for their lil' relationship because while I was out during the day Cyn was there to keep Erin company as they did whatever the hell it was at that shop. I never understood what was so fascinating about sitting around in the hair salon all day. I swear all they did was bump their gums and talk about how niggas wasn't shit.

"Wassup, Money."

"My nigga, why do I have to call you five times before you answer? You still ducking Niecy's ass?" Tevin was real life scared of Shaniece. She had him changing phone numbers and looking over his shoulders whenever he was in the streets.

"Man, that shit ain't funny you know her ass popped up on me the other night while I was at the shop trying to talk some real shit to Cyn. I swear it was like Déjà Vu with sis there. E was about three seconds from getting in that ass, but she got this counting shit she do now to calm her down and shit."

"Yeah she told me about that. I would've kicked your ass if you had my lady out there fighting over your drama."

"Man, Lia, is your damn lady. E don't belong to you." On some real shit, I had to stare at the phone for a good minute because it couldn't have been my nigga on the other end of the phone throwing shade like that.

"Say that. Where you at, though? I'm about to pull up on you." When Tevin told me his location I hung up on that ass. Why he said half the shit he did out his mouth was beyond me. If he wasn't my family I'd think that nigga was jealous, but Tevin was my man a hunned grand, and just like me he was cut from a different cloth. After my granny passed, Tevin was all I had before I met E.

I was nine when my parents were deported back to Jamaica and my granny was left to raise me. My granny was dope as fuck, but when she was diagnosed with cancer when I was fourteen shit started changing for us. Bills started piling up and I started making runs for this older dude in the hood named Gregory. Gregory was a fat, lazy motherfucker, and at the time, Tevin was known as a jack boy and I would say wassup to him in passing. We chilled together whenever he decided to come to school because we were from the same building. After three months of working for Gregory, some older dude approached me about a way to get fifteen bands. I had to choose one person to help me get rid of Gregory, and the only person I knew at the time that was real right was Tevin. Tevin put the fear of God in a lot of people twice our age, and his ass didn't care about anything. I knew from the moment we met it was either we were going to be cool or at each other's throat. We both chose the latter and ever since we packed Gregory's thieving ass up, Tee and I had been getting money together ever since. It was crazy how everything started falling into place after Gregory was gone. Tevin and I became lieutenants at this trap on Claritin, and I met E and shit had been lit for us because she came and leveled both of our asses up. I never expected E to be that piece to the puzzle to help Tevin and I get up out the hood, but she was. Her hunger to not want to go back to her boujee ass family was what drove us to grind harder, along with my love for her. I wanted E to have everything her heart desired because she deserved it. She went to school, kept straight A's, and still made time to make sure my shit was in order, too. Her main concern was surviving after leaving a very sheltered life and exposing herself to the harsh reality of the streets. E was hungry and the little bit of money she had wasn't going to cut it and she knew that. When E came along, I finally had someone to care about other than myself. She changed the way I saw life and CK respected that because his lady did the same for him. I think he low-key rocked with E more than he did me, and I didn't even mind because if it wasn't for her none of this shit would have been possible. Now at twenty-four years old, my niggas and I had all six boroughs and neighboring cities on lock with the best product flooding the streets. A lot of niggas counted me out after my parents got deported and my granny passed. Hell, even I ain't believe I was going to be shit, but look at me now with over fifteen mil stacked up and money flowing.

When I pulled up on Tevin, he was standing out front chopping it up with some Spanish chick that I had never seen before. Tevin was about six-foot-six and 195 pounds soaking wet. He was a real pretty boy, one that was ruthless as hell if need be. His choice of women always concerned me, because even as he was dying to get Cyn back, he was still on the same little kid shit that caused him to lose her, but that wasn't my place to tell the next man how to live his life. I looked to Cyn like a sister and

I hated to see her get dogged by my boy when I knew deep down she was where he wanted to be. Tevin was just too caught up to realize the shit, but whenever he got a little liquor in his system his ass was sick and in his feelings about Cyn. Alcohol brought out the worst in motherfuckers; that's why I did my best to know my limits. Tevin had always been my guideline for what not to do because his ass was so damn reckless. It was like after Cyn caught him with Shaniece, it was a wrap for that ass and sis ain't look back. No matter how much he begged and pleaded, Cyn stuck to her guns and was focused on getting to that bag. She reminded me so much of E; I think that's why I fucked with her the long way, and E being away just brought us closer. After running around for the past year and a half, Tevin was finally realizing that Cyn was the one for him, but she wasn't on the same page and the shit was driving him crazy.

"What's good, baby." I dapped Tee up once he finished chopping it up with his home girl. I don't know what I would do if E ever decided that she wasn't fucking with me anymore. I know for sure I'd probably fuck her and any nigga she thought she was gonna replace me with up for a fact.

"Bra, wassup with Cyn? I know E be telling your ass everything and Cyn tells her ass everything. Whenever I try to get up with her, sis is always around. Since when their asses became frick and frack?"

"Tee, man, I don't even know why you do this to yourself, bra. She good though; her and E go back from high school and the building. You knew it was only a matter of time before they picked up right where they left off."

"Yeah, aiigh, I'm trying to get her ass back, but she ain't been trying to give a nigga no play. Cyn was my heart and I fucked that up chasing after Niecy's crazy ass." We headed into the house, and after collecting my money, I was ready to go home. Ever since E came home, I found myself wanting to be in the house more and more. Once I dropped this off to my stash house, that not even Tevin knew about, I was heading home to my baby.

My phone started ringing once I pulled up to the stash house I had in L.I. As I fished in my pocket for my phone, I smiled thinking it was E calling, but my smile grew even bigger once I realized who was on the other end of the call.

"Good afternoon, Mama." I greeted my mother. I hadn't heard from her in a few months and I was glad she was calling. My parents were back in Jamaica living out their lives, while their only son was here living the not so American dream.

"Kymani, good afternoon, son. Your father wanted me to call and check on you. We know Erin was released. How is that beautiful woman, and when are you going to bring her and my grandbaby to visit?" Unlike Talia, my parents loved Erin.

"Soon, mama, real soon." My mother's accent was evident, but the small time she spent in America and the many trips she and my father made here before I was even born helped her out a lot. "Did you and dad get the money I sent for you?" My father took it as a sign of disrespect that I sent him and my mom so much money, so I only sent money on birthdays and holidays, so that he wouldn't think much of it.

"Yeah, we got it, but you know your father, Kymani. He doesn't want, nor need, your money. You being alive and well is payment enough for the both of us. We've been putting that money aside for our grandbaby. We are fine, son." I knew my father was well off in his own right, but I just wanted to repay him for all that he's done for me. Growing up poor in a small village in the heart of Jamaica added to the hunger I had to succeed and do right by my family.

"Ok, son, I have to go; your father says hello. Tell Azia we love her and Erin we send our love. I hope we get to see you guys soon. Be careful, Kymani. I love you." I could hear the sadness in my mother's voice, and I wished I could just have her here in the states with me.

"I love you more, my queen," I told her before hanging up the phone. It was always a great feeling speaking to my mother, even though my father was always too stubborn to get on the phone. I grabbed the two duffle bags and entered the house. There was a vault in the floor of the back room where I held my money. I hadn't gotten around to counting it in a while and I wasn't looking forward to doing so today being that I told E I would be home at a decent hour. If I started counting, I'd be here for hours. I did keep a log of how much I deposited each time, but I always had to count to double check. I closed the vault and locked up the house.

Lia: *I miss you, daddy.*

A part of me wanted to make a detour and go slide up in her shit, but I had something way better waiting for me at home. I couldn't even compare the two if I wanted because E and Lia were total opposites. The only thing that attracted me to Talia was her looks and the twenty-four-hour access I had to her. It could be three in the morning and she'd be dead sleep, but if I came over she was ready and willing by the time I hit the top step. Damn, I was gonna miss that shit.

Chapter Four

Cyn

Tonight, we were surprising E with a welcome home party in the city. There were so many people here to show love to E, and I know her anti-social ass was probably giving Ky a hard time right now getting ready. Every second she was texting asking if I knew what Ky had planned, and when I didn't respond her ass started sending threats. I don't know what it was but Future's songs always went hard in the club. "Stick Talk" was playing as I sat in VIP waiting for the guest of honor to arrive. I wasn't a fan of surprises, but E lived for shit like that and everyday Ky came home with something for her. I adored their relationship and the way he treated her.

I didn't expect half the people to show up because E had been gone for five whole years, but a lot of people fucked with her and Ky the long way. E was that ride or die chick that every trap nigga wished they could have, but Ky lucked up and snatched her up. In high school I was probably the only female E messed with, so the female turnout was based solely on Tevin and Ky's hoeness. Every bitch in New York wanted to be wherever their asses were, but me and my bitch already had those spots solidified. I could front all I wanted, but I loved Tevin down to his dirty draws.

When E got locked up, for weeks I watched Ky walk around with his head held low and I knew for a fact had she been home or able to see him in this state she would've got in his ass for blaming himself for her current situation, so I stepped in and made sure everything went according to the plans they had. Ky didn't know, but I was the only person that E told about her family's involvement with the FBI. That's how E was able to know about the raid beforehand because her uncle was on the same task force that was put together to come and sweep her and Ky's crib. E and I had been rocking since the tenth grade, but now we're closer than we've ever been. Since she's been home I was able to see the Erin that Kymani fell in love with, E was a whole fool for real and everything about her was genuine. There was no way you couldn't love her ass.

CK and his wife, Alana, were even in attendance. I've only heard stories about the infamous Alana and to see her in person I was taken back by her beauty. Like she was drop dead gorgeous and nothing like I imagined this hood legend to be. All Erin did was talk about Alana; it was Alana this and Alana that. E looked to Alana like a mother, and the way she spoke so highly of Erin from the small conversation we had, I could tell the feelings were mutual. Kymani and Erin were the modern day CK and Alana. I wasn't sure where Tevin fit into the equation because it was always just CK and Alana, and they ran everything together. But Ky and Tevin had a history neither me or Erin understood because they were total opposites, but we all loved Tevin's crazy ass.

I watched on in amazement as Alana and CK sat there enjoying one another's company without a care in the world. I wished like hell Tevin would get himself together so that we could shit on these niggas and bitches just like them. The lap dance CK was getting from the big booty stripper didn't seem to bother Alana one bit. Their shit seemed so secure as she tossed hundreds and fifties over the stripper's body while she danced for her man. I was so afraid to give Tevin another chance because the first time hurt so bad when he broke my heart with his whorish ways. His dark brown eyes and curly tapered fade gave me P. Diddy's son, Justin, all the time. Only thing was Tevin was way taller at six-foot-six. He was looking hella good in his ripped jeans and off-white sweatshirt topped off with a pair of black 9" Timberlands. I was going to keep my distance or else Tevin was going to end up in my bed, and I would regret the shit in the morning because he was still on his same high school shit. There were so many other niggas dying to get with me, but my dumb ass was stuck on stupid. Tevin Marquis Daniels. I saw that he was trying to behave after I showed my ass the last time he tried to flaunt one of his freaks of the week in my face. I wanted to settle down with Tevin and build a family with his dumb ass but I wasn't about to subject myself to the bullshit that came along with being with him. If there was one thing my mother taught me before she checked out and left me to raise myself was that a nigga only did what you allowed him to, and if I kept taking Tevin back while he was still playing games then his ass was going to continue to do me wrong.

"We got New York's finest in the building and I'm not talking them boys in blue. My nigga, Money, and the first lady are in the building. Welcome home, E." The DJ announced their arrival over the mic and Alana's smile was contagious as we all watched Erin make her way through the sea of people. Her and Ky stopped to speak to a few people before they made it to our section, and when they did that's when the water works started. I was glad E wasn't a fan of makeup because if she was her face would have been ruined once she laid eyes on Alana.

"Baby boy, wass good?" CK stood and embraced in a brotherly hug with Ky as Alana and Erin held on to one another for dear life. Alana was about ten maybe fifteen years older than us, and she didn't look a day over twenty. I was happy Alana was here because now E had no reason to leave with her here.

"Welcome home, E, glad you're back. This nigga been messing up the count ever since you got knocked," CK joked as he hugged Erin.

"Keep talking, old man, and I'll buy Alana a new house with your cut so she can get away from your old ass."

"Thank you, CK. It's good to be back. I'm so happy y'all are here."

"We wouldn't miss this for anything, Daughty, even though Kymani gave us the wrong address. If it wasn't for this beauty we would have been at the wrong location," Alana said talking in my direction.

"Aww, Cyn, this is my Ma, the Muva of all mothers. Ma, this is Cynthia, Tevin's girl and my only friend."

"Any friend of Daughty's is good enough for me because it's not every day Erin talks my ear off about someone other than Ky. So, now that we're all acquainted, let's turn up," Alana yelled as she motioned for the bottle

71

service girls to come over. Tevin was standing to the left of me and I discreetly whispered in his ear letting him know to not show his ass tonight if he planned on drinking. Alana's energy was crazy though and we were all having a good time in VIP celebrating my bitch being home. Erin, Alana, and I enjoyed a few lap dances from the dancers that were in our sections as we blew a bag on them and sang along to the popping ass songs the DJ was spinning tonight. Tevin, CK, Ky, and their crew were off to the side, blowing dope and catching the eye of every female in the spot. I sent a few dancers over there to keep them entertained before a bitch got the guts to step to any one of them. I didn't have time to show my ass tonight, and I knew firsthand how E gave it up and nobody had time for her crazy ass.

I could feel Tevin watching me as I danced with Erin while some random chick danced up on him. Shawty was busted and wasn't even worth my energy and I knew me not reacting would piss Tevin off more than anything because just like a child, he did shit for attention.

"You two need to get a room. I see how that boy is looking at you," Alana said over the music. I shyly smiled because I didn't think anyone was paying us any attention, but I was wrong because her and Erin both found amusement in Tevin and I.

"I'm not thinking about that boy."

"And a boy he is, but you're definitely thinking about him. Don't worry he'll get himself together soon. It took for me and Cedrick to go through hell and back in order to get where we are today. Everybody can't get it right on the first try like Erin and Kymani." Alana laughed as she nudged Erin.

"Hey, you said it, not me. But for real Ky and I aren't perfect we just love hard as hell and nothing or no one can come in between that." I heard the sincerity in Erin's voice as Ky and the guys made their way over to us.

"What y'all over here talking about?" Ky asked.

"Nothing, babe. Gimmie kiss." Seeing E and Alana all booed up had me in my feelings so I was going to take a much-needed trip to the bathroom. Tevin was still over there entertaining that whack bitch and my blood was boiling.

"Fuck, Tevin." I know no one heard me, but it felt good to say aloud. I've never disrespected Tevin the way he did me. I hated the way I cared for him, I would forever be in my feelings until Cynthia wasn't the only one that cared for there to be a Tevin and Cyn.

While I was in the bathroom washing my hands, I could see E standing behind me. I wasn't paying her ass any mind though because if I did I knew I was going to go in about Tevin, and tonight was her night; I could cry to her about Tevin tomorrow night.

"Cyn, you want me to talk to him? Because I will. Tevin is just acting out because you're not ready to take him back yet, or are you?"

"Sis, tonight is about you; not me and your dumb ass brother. I'm cool on Tevin for real. As long as that bitch is gone by the time I get back up there, I'm good."

When we got back upstairs, E whispered something in Ky's ear and he made his way over to where Tevin and the chick were standing. I could tell by the scowl on Tevin's face that the conversation wasn't going his way, but I was satisfied once ol' girl made her way towards the stairs. Still Tevin didn't come to sit with us, but that was okay, too. His dumb ass could stay over there all he wanted as long as he was by himself.

In my tight fitted body suit, I knew I looked good because the way my thighs filled up the fabric had every man in their right mind staring and wishing they were the ones dancing up on me besides Erin. My home girl, Naya, laid my hair with my thirty-two-inch install. A bitch couldn't tell me anything. I lived for a side part and long ass weave; twenty-eight-inches was the shortest I've ever went. I was most definitely feeling myself now that Tevin was the one in his feelings. I wasn't sure how he planned on getting me back doing the corny shit that he was into, but that wasn't my focus. Right now, E wanted to turn up, so that's what we were about to do. Those five years did nothing to E because she was still one of the baddest and you could tell she took good care of herself while locked up. Most people come home worst off than they went in because they allowed the stress of being locked up get to them. With a five-year bid, I'd probably lose my mind day one. E was a different breed for real; she made that shit look so easy.

We were all up in VIP enjoying ourselves as we danced along to the music. E and Alana were out there like they had no care in the world and I wasn't no bitter bitch; I was just sexually frustrated and deprived so my happiness seemed like third place compared to the way they were glowing and carrying on with their men. I always knew Erin loved to dance, and the way she was throwing it back on Ky let everyone else know it, too. The few shots of Patron that I took were starting to sneak up on me along with the good weed I had gotten a taste of from CK moments ago. I was feeling it as I began to move my hips along to the music. I was in my own little world as I danced like I was in the comfort of my own home and not in a club full of thirsty niggas and the craziest one that I was in love with. When some dude came up and danced behind me, I thought nothing of it because we were in a club and I was free to dance with whomever I wanted. *Right.*

Rhianna's "Work" played as I danced up on this stranger.

Work, work, work, work, work, work

You see me I be work, work, work, work, work, work,

You see me do me dirt, dirt, dirt, dirt, dirt

There's something 'bout that work, work, work, work, work

When you a gon' learn, learn. Learn, learn, learn

Me na care if me tired, tired, tired, tired, tired

Join me I deserve it

No time to have you lurking

If I go right then you might like it

You know I dealt with the nicest

I was enjoying myself and happy that Mr. Man could keep up with me. Usually I had to ditch my dance partner's mid-song because they weren't able to keep up. I peeped Tevin watching us, but I didn't care. He could have his fun; why couldn't I? But when he pushed himself off the wall, I just knew it was about to be some shit. I slowed down my movement and tried my best to move away from my dance partner before Tevin came over here showing his ass.

"You really think I'm a fucking joke, Cyn," Tevin said through gritted teeth as he grabbed me by the arm and pushed me down on the couch. This nigga was real life crazy. I don't even know why I played myself.

Tevin hauled off on the dude and surprisingly ol' boy ain't back down and he was giving Tevin a run for his money until his ass went bonkers. Tevin had busted the dude's lip and nose with one punch.

"Tevin, okay enough. We were just dancing; what the fuck is wrong with you?" I was yelling and screaming and Tevin seemed unphased. I never understood why Tevin did half the shit he did. We weren't together, so why he chose to show his ass over a dance was beyond me.
When Tevin didn't answer, I took it upon myself to pull him off the dude since Ky and CK were acting like they didn't see shit. I knew Tevin wasn't dumb enough to hit me because I wasn't afraid to hit his retarded ass back. After popping him

upside his head a few times, Tevin wrapped me up in his massive arms making it hard for me to move for more reasons than one. His touch always did something to me and the way his chest rose and fell against mine had me thinking back to all the times he would hold me in his arms before we went to bed. Tevin was fine as hell and he knew it, and as much as I wanted to be mad at his ass, I was caught up in the smell of his cologne and being this close to him. It had been so long since I felt his touch.

Tevin was real life crazy and I had seen him show his ass for less than this. There were times when he would go off on somebody for even looking at him the wrong way. He went zero to one hundred in less than sixty seconds and would be cool sixty seconds after that. Tevin and I's chemistry was undeniable because to the outside looking in one would think we were this happy couple enjoying one another's company rather than this being the hostile moment that it was.

"Tevin, what the fuck? You can dish it out, but when it's done to you, your ass is in here showing your ass."

"Fuck all that, Cyn. Your ass is in here playing disrespect like I won't fuck you and that nigga up. That's ya man now? That nigga is the reason you won't answer my calls and shit." Yeah, this man's elevator didn't go all the way up for sure. He knew I didn't know that man from anywhere and while security picked him up off the floor I shook my head because this shit was unnecessary.

"Let me go, Tevin."

"Nah, fuck that, Cyn. You know I don't play with your ass. Why would you even think I would sit back and let the next nigga dance up on what's mine."

"I don't fucking belong to your ass. Did you see me showing my ass when you were over there entertaining that bitch? Exactly. I can't control your disrespectful ass, so I don't know why you're even tripping right now." From where we were standing I could see E and Alana still dancing and enjoying themselves while I was left to deal with Tevin and all his crazy. I was going to fuck Ky up because his ass found the shit hilarious. Usually Ky was the one who had my back and stopped Tevin from showing his ass.

"Man, I don't even be out here as much as you think I do. You giving a nigga way too much credit. Your ass doesn't wanna be with me, so what you expect me to do?" His voice was now more stern as he spoke directly to me rather than yelling and making a scene.

"Fight; I want you to fight for me, Tevin, damn. Do I not deserve that much? You show your ass on the regular, bitch after bitch, and you wonder why we can't be together. I love you, Tevin, and you keep playing with my feelings like they mean nothing to you." I hated that we were having this conversation right here, right now but fuck it.

"Don't cry, ma. I love you too. Just give me another chance to get my shit together. I promise all this shit just been to get you to look at a nigga. I miss you, Cyn." I wanted to believe Tevin, but it wasn't that easy. This wasn't the first time he'd professed his love to me.

"I gotta go, Tevin. Let me go please." I could feel myself about to give in as the tears fell down my cheeks and I wasn't trying to do this right here because I wanted to believe him so that we could leave here together and live happily ever after, but that was farfetched. We've both been drinking, and if he was serious about us he'd feel the same way in the morning or whenever we revisited this conversation.

I slipped out of Tevin's grasped as he loosened his grip on me and went to say my goodbyes to E and Alana. I hope this little fiasco didn't ruin Alana's perception of me because I really liked her. She was someone you wanted to like you back being that she was a boss ass bitch, one that I aspired to be.

"I'll call you, Cyn. Text me when you get in. I'll make sure Tevin doesn't follow your ass home," E joked while I thanked God because that's exactly what his ass probably planned on doing.

"Damn, I don't get no love, sis?" Ky laughed as I hugged CK then Alana good bye, leaving his ass standing there.

"I couldn't get no help with your crazy ass friend, so no. Later brother, love ya," I shouted over my shoulder as I made my way downstairs and through the doors of the club. The slight breeze gave me a calming feeling as I waited for the driver to open my door. There was no way I was driving to the city plus I was still a little buzzed.

***

It had been a week since E's welcome home party, and with Erin out of town with Alana, I've been so lonely. They extended the invitation, but I had back to back appointments all week and it would have been fucked up if I canceled on them like that. Thanksgiving was approaching and I didn't need any of my clients bashing me on social media and shit.

I had just got off FaceTime with E and Alana and they seemed to be having so much fun without me. I was low-key jealous because here I was in the house curled up with my full-length body pillow, catching up on Grey's Anatomy. I was so happy that E was home because growing up, it had always been just me. My mom was on that shit, and there wasn't a day I could remember that we didn't argue or fight. Talani was an abusive ass parent and the reason I fought my way through high school. My mother never took the time to get to know me or even talk to me. Since I was old enough to work, she had her hand out looking for me to dish out my small summer youth checks to support her habit of tricking on little ass boys. My mother had a thing for younger men and it drove me crazy because most of her boyfriends were so close to my age and the real dumb ones still went to Jeff with me. I used to get teased every day because my mom would come up to the school and show her ass arguing with girl's half her age, and I would end up having to fight them because there was no way I was letting them jump my mother. After four years of going through every available senior and junior, my mother finally let go of her cradle robbing habits and up and moved to North Carolina with the pastor from our church. I thanked God every day for Pastor because he saved my mother's life for sure. Without him, she'd probably be dead or in jail for messing with the wrong person's son or boyfriend. Pastor offered my mom something she had never had before and that was love and learning to love herself before anyone else. I guess I turned out okay because I used my mother's actions as what not to do. I wanted to win too bad to end up like Talani. Even now with her having her life together, I still wanted nothing to do with her. I've done just fine without her and I think my past was the reason I was so hard on Tevin. I was so afraid of falling in love with him only for him to up and leave me like my father did my mom, and I end up losing my marbles just like her ass.

After watching yet another episode of Grey's Anatomy, I checked the time and realized it was only a little after eight and my stomach was on the gate. I had eaten a late lunch when I was at the shop, so when I got home a few hours ago, I wasn't hungry. But now after smoking a fat ass blunt, I had the munchies. Footprints wasn't too far from my house and some Rasta Pasta didn't sound half bad as long as they put extra barbeque sauce, I was straight. I threw on my

PINK sweat suit and slides and headed to Footprints on Flatbush; the one on Claritin stayed packed, and I was trying to pick up my food and be gone. When I pulled up I was happy that there wasn't a long wait because I felt like they moved extra slow when there was a lot of people in here, and this shit was supposed to be express. I was watching them like a hawk because I asked for extra barbeque sauce and every time they charged me, but never put it in the bag. When I felt someone come up behind me, I clutched my mace ready to let them have it because when I walked in there a few chicks were staring me up and down, and I didn't have the energy to fight. They were gonna get maced the fuck up and I was going to go on about my damn business.

"You gon' mace me, Cynny." I smelt him before I even heard him, but I still didn't let go of the grip on my mace just in case Tevin was still on that bullshit. He lived for public shows and stuff like that. When I turned around, I was faced with the biggest smile and open arms. I hadn't seen Tevin since that night at the club, and I wasn't sure if I wanted to be mad at him or fall right into his arms, so I chose the latter and turned back to the register after I looked him up and down. He was looking extra good in his

Nike joggers and hoodie though, I swear Tevin wore the shit out of a sweat suit. He knew I hated it when he wore that shit outside because it was a thirst trap for these bitches. The smirk he wore on his face told me that he knew exactly what I was thinking and I didn't like it one bit.

"Cyn, I said I was sorry; we talked about that shit. Why you still giving me the cold shoulder, ma?"

"Order 358, 356." The cashier yelled out as she eyed Tevin and I hard. Yeah, I needed to get the fuck out of here before I caught a case. I pulled my bank card from out my Louie wallet and proceeded to pay for my food.

"Don't disrespect me like that, Cyn. You can put them together, ma." The way the chick was eye fucking him was irritating the shit out of me because his ass was just too damn friendly.

"No, don't disrespect me like that, Marquis. Thanks for the food though; I'll see you." I grabbed my food and made my way to the door and I could hear the cashier suck her teeth.

"Damn, Cyn, why you treating a nigga like this? I can't even get a thank you."

"I told you I could pay for my own food, Tevin. Could you move this big shit so I can go, please?" I didn't park too far so I was already at my car, and Tevin was blocking me in with his truck.

"I know you could pay for your own food. When you gon' stop being mean to me? I said sorry over a thousand times."

"Tevin, I don't wanna do this right now. We have this conversation all the time, and still when we are somewhere together, bitches are way too comfortable around you. You know what my problem is and you're still Mr. Fucking Friendly."

"I don't care about them bitches, Cyn, and you know that the only bit... female I care about is your ass."

"Tevin, come on. I wanna go home and eat my food. Why you so pressed over me when you have a whole fan club of bitches?" I nodded my head towards the two chicks that were standing outside.

"I'm where I wanna be, Cyn. Stop bringing up irrelevant shit." He was right. It was like every other conversation we had, I was bringing up other bitches.

"Since you paid for my food the least I could do is keep you company while you eat. I'll follow you to the house." I wasn't bringing Tevin back to my house because his ass probably wasn't going to leave. That million-dollar smile appeared again and the wall I had built around my heart began to crumble a little.

"Nah, I'm gonna follow your ass. You still know the way, right?" he sarcastically asked as he opened my door for me and waited until I was securely inside. It took me like fifteen minutes to get to Tevin's house and he pulled up a few minutes after me. He could never keep up with me. When we used to race home, he used to come up off a few bands because I always won. When we walked inside I smiled because everything was just how I left it.

"Even in the Wrangler I still beat you home," I joked as we both washed our hands at the kitchen sink.

"I let your ass win." I gave him that 'nigga you know you lying' look and sat down on top of the counter and opened my food up. We were so into our food that all you could hear was Tevin's smacking and the scraping of our forks against the tin containers. The picture of Tevin and me from our first date to the city was still hanging on his refrigerator where I first hung it up.

"I see not much has changed." I hopped off the counter and moved around the front of the house freely as Tevin fired up the blunt that set next to the many pre-rolled blunts on the table. Instead of replying, he sat down on the olive green sectional and patted the spot next to him as he pulled from the blunt. I knew if I smoked I was going to be knocked out, but Ky and Tevin had that fye and I was a low-key weed head now after being with Tevin for two years.

I hooked my phone up to his speakers and let my SoundCloud playlist play as he sat there blowing smoke in the air. I went to grab the blunt from him and Tevin pulled me down next to him.

"Why you acting like you don't wanna be next to me, Cyn? I know you miss me," he spoke into the crook of my neck as I tried to move away from him. I paid him no mind as I inhaled the thick cloud.

"I see you're still reading." I pointed out as I scrolled through the Kindle App on his iPad. He was caught up on all the latest too. I made a mental note to check some of them out for myself. I was trying to busy myself because being this close to him in the house we used to share was doing something to me and definitely had me feeling some type of way. Tevin was the only street nigga I was into and I used to tell myself to never fall in love with a hustla, but here I was four years later still in love with his dusty ass. I could feel him staring me down, but I wasn't trying to look up just yet because if I did all those ill feelings would be out the window. Everything about this moment seemed right; nothing felt forced and I wasn't uncomfortable being this close to him.

"Yeah you know I love me a good hood book. I feel like they be talking to a nigga for real." He was so close to me that I could feel his cool breath on my neck with every word he spoke. His phone rang and he didn't even bother looking at it and that told me it had to be one of his bitches. Unwillingly, I sucked my teeth and moved over towards the edge of the couch.

"It ain't nobody but Ky. Him and E the only ones with my number. I told you I'm not on that shit anymore, Cyn. A nigga been chilling for the past few months; anytime you saw me with a chick was just to get your ass to notice me. I know I was wrong, but it worked." I rolled my eyes and passed the blunt back to him as he looked me in my eyes. He was so damn petty. Instead of having a regular conversation, Tevin wanted to be petty.

"Whatever, Marquis." I sat back on the couch and closed my eyes, enjoying my high. When I felt Tevin's lips on my neck, I wanted to say something but when his lips covered mine there was nothing left to say. His lips were still sweet to me and as our tongues danced around I felt his hands pull my legs under him on the couch. I tried to pull back, but he had a hold on my lip with his teeth as he tugged on my bottom lip and devoured it with his massive lips. As much as I wanted to seem uninterested, a soft moan escaped my lips. I missed this, and if he kept it up, tonight just might be his lucky night. I was sexually frustrated and his touch alone caused me to squirm beneath him. Flashbacks of our many sexcapades on this very couch played in my head. When he broke our kiss, disappointment was written all over my face as he smiled down at me.

"You not fucking with me, right?" his dumb ass had the nerve to say. Well that's what his mouth was saying, but the bulge in his pants was telling me everything I needed.

"Nope, but I am fucking you tonight." I laughed at my own corny ass line and Tevin resumed what he was doing and that was making love to my neck and mouth. This was long overdue and I was just about to show him how much I wasn't fucking with him.

Chapter Five

Erin

"Your ass looks guilty as fuck." I had been blowing Cyn's phone up for the past two days. Alana and I had ended our mini vacation a day early due to Ky and CK blowing us up every hour. I had been looking for Cynthia's ass for the past two days. Ky would laugh whenever I asked for her and said she was under the weather or some weak shit like that.

"I was sick." The goofy look on her face told me that she wasn't telling the truth and she had that 'I just got some' glow to her that I knew all too well since I've been home.

"My brother is going to fuck you and that nigga up. I hope you know what you're getting yourself into." I was team Tevin all day every day. Not because Tevin was family but because of the way she looked at him and smiled every time she talked about him even when he pissed her off.

"Well I hope his ass is as good at shadowboxing as he is at... never mind." I hated that 'never mind' shit that her and Kymani did. I wasn't hipped to the new slang at all.

"I knew, you nasty bitch. Tell me everything. Do I need to put my wedding planning skills into effect or what?"

"Only if Ky proposed and your ass didn't feel the need to tell me."

"I don't need a wedding to know that my nigga is mine; Kymani ain't going no damn where. Tevin, on the other hand, he needs stability and something to look forward to, to calm his wild ass down." I did think of marriage often, but that was something Ky and I never talked about after he proposed to me with a ring pop when we were seventeen like Norbit did with Kate in the movie.

"Well okay, bitch. Anyway, Tevin and I are just figuring some stuff out right now. I'm not about to put my all into him yet again only to get my heart broken. We could save the wedding planning for the day we go a week without wanting to kill one another.

"Fine," I sadly said as I pouted. I was rooting for them though because Cyn deserved to be loved properly and Tevin needed Cyn. She kept his ass leveled.

"I'm gonna call you later. I told Ky I would be right back. Cyn, don't have me looking for your ass like this again thanks, boo." I had to pop up on her ass at the shop because Cyn knew I didn't play with her. Let me not answer my phone after the first ring and she was at my door.

Faith in my Hustla

I decided to drive my G-wagon today because Ky drove his earlier, and I thought it was cute how people stopped to snap pictures of us whenever we pulled up in the same ride. Nine times out of ten, Kymani was copying me because I was always the first one ready. Ever since we met, Ky found the need to dress like me, he always wanted to match my fly. At fifteen, I was the definition of a tomboy and all through high school, up until my senior year, it was nothing but jeans and sneakers for me. That's why it was so easy for Ky and I to dress alike. But as I neared the end of my junior year, I started developing body parts I thought I'd never have, like ass and titties. The more my body began to spread the more I began to embrace my figure and dressed accordingly. As much as Kymani complained about the clothes I wore, his ass loved it, but he could do without the extra attention it brought me. Ky made sure to let it be known to everyone in our neighborhood and my school that I was his and whoever felt the need to play disrespect caught these hands by either him or me depending on how I was feeling that day. Since fifteen, I only had eyes for Kymani, well except for that whole Robert phase I had. Robert was the star player on the varsity basketball team and out of all the girls in our school, he only had eyes for me and I loved the attention I got throughout the school day. Ky was two years older than me, so he had already graduated and Robert was my school boo. It was all harmless, but Kymani wasn't here for none of that shit and he let it be known after him and Robert fought on countless occasions. It got to the point where Robert wouldn't even speak to me, and whenever Cyn and I would go to the games to see him play, he'd act like I wasn't even there because of Kymani's crazy ass.

When Alana offered to take me to Miami I was elated, I look to Alana like a mother and since I was fifteen she always held it down. When I needed to vent she was there; when I needed someone to come and talk to the teachers at my school about college she was there; prom, graduation she was there. Alana had been more of a mother to me in the years I've known her than my birth mom. Kymani was the gift in my life that kept on giving because if it wasn't for him, I'd still be miserable due to the life my parents had planned for me since the day I was born. Ky brought me so much love and happiness from day one when I was standing outside the shelter on 145th and Farmers. I didn't want to go to Miami without Ky, but him and CK had their own business to tend to, so I guess our little trip was to keep us out of their way while they handled their business. Being away from Ky for a whole week had me love sick, I was so used to being up under him when I went to bed, that when our trip was cut short, I didn't even complain.

"E, you heard me." Ky's voice startled me as I pulled into the driveway of our home. I had forgotten that he was on FaceTime being that I was so caught up in my thoughts.

"Sorry, bae, I didn't hear you. I'm pulling up to the house now though. It'll only take me an hour to shower and get dressed. I promise I'll be ready when you get home." I played myself popping up on Cyn knowing Ky made plans for us today, but I had to make sure my bitch was alive and well. I couldn't take Ky's word for it after what happened between her and Tevin at the club that night. Tonight was all about me and my baby, so I pushed the many thoughts of everything but Ky to the back of my mind and made my way in the house to get ready. While I busied myself in my closet, that turned out being Ky's closet too because his ass felt like mine was big enough for the both of us, I let Mary J play in the back while I decided on something to wear. Ky wouldn't tell me where we were going, but he told me to dress comfortable and sent me a picture of his outfit so I could dress accordingly. Once I settled on an outfit almost similar to Ky's, I was satisfied and hoped the water was nice and hot how I liked it. I always let the water run before I showered because I loved the steamy effect it gave the bathroom. I wrapped my hair up and covered it with a bonnet and shower cap and undressed. When the water hit my body, I began to relax and allowed the one-thousand-dollar showerhead to do its job. The water pressure was amazing and it did the job every trip.

When I heard the bathroom door open, then shut, I smiled knowing Kymani was going to make his way home when I mentioned that I had to shower. I hadn't taken a shower yet in this house without him. The way his hands maneuvered their way around my body as he washed me up was a feeling I had grown used to. I was spoiled and it was all his fault. I slid the shower door back allowing him access once he was fully undressed and welcomed his massive arms around my small frame. We stood under the showerhead in each other's arms, enjoying the steam filled moment as Ky watched me hungrily and his throbbing manhood poked me just below my bellybutton. I was looking forward to the orgasmic rollercoaster he was sure to take me on as his hands traveled from my waist to my breast. There were no words that needed to be spoken as we let our bodies do all the talking for us. I slipped my tiny hands down and massaged his third leg as he bent down and placed kisses from my head to my chest. My breasts were always my most vulnerable spot since the day Ky and I first had sex. Every time he would lick, suck, and tug on them, or even the slightest touch, I went crazy. The way he French kissed my breast had me anticipating what was to come next as he used his freehand to rub his dick against my now wet clit. I could tell Ky was growing tired of the four play, but did it because he knew I enjoyed it and it always got me in the mood. When he tried to enter me, I looked at him puzzled because he knew there was no way he could stick it without licking it.

"Your ass is spoiled," he hissed as he trailed kisses from my chest and stopped at my dripping wet center. I held on to the rail in the shower as Ky placed my legs on his shoulders and pleased me with his monster tongue. I held myself up on the rail and used my freehand to help guide his head in deeper. Ky was playing with it and I couldn't take it as his tongue brushed up against my clit a few times

"Kymani," I whined and he looked up at me and winked with a smirk on his beautiful face. I loved everything about Ky and I couldn't picture life without him, Kymani was my first everything and I planned on keeping it that way. Ky hungrily attacked my clit and my words were cut short; he didn't stop until my juices were flowing down the sides of his mouth.

"I'm cummin', Kyyy! Ohhhh, fuckkkk!" I removed my hand from the back of his head and covered my mouth in an attempt to muffle my screams. Kymani always got big headed when I started yelling.

"Kymani!" I screamed because he had a hold on my waist as I tried to get down. I couldn't take anymore; my body had just finished convulsing. He turned the shower off and carried me to our bedroom. The window was open as always because Ky couldn't function without there being a breeze of some kind in our room. The cool air felt good against my naked, wet body as Ky placed me on the bed on my stomach. I damn near tore a hole in the sheets when he entered me from behind. I buried my head in the plush sheets to muffle my screams.

"Nah, let that shit out, ma. I want the neighbors to know my name," he groaned as he dug deeper. We had sex on the regular and still, I wasn't used to his size. Kymani was way bigger than he was five years ago and I was loving the shit.

Faith in my Hustla

"Damn, Ky, that's my spot."

"I know." He cockily smiled as I looked back at him and watched him thrust in and out of me, hitting my spot over and over. I couldn't let him out do me, so I threw my ass back matching him stroke for stroke as I sucked on my bottom lip. I was trying to get him to nut first, so I gripped myself on his dick and went to work. His once fast paced movements were slowed as he gripped my waist tightly. I wanted to watch him from a better angle, so I swiftly turned around making sure to keep him still inside me. That was one of the many perks of being pint sized.

"Fuck, E! Baby!" he moaned as he laid on top of me. I nudged him a little so that he could roll over and I could be on top. Playtime was over and I was about to show his ass who was boss. The look on his face brought a devilish grin to my face as he laid there with his eyes closed while I rode him to ecstasy. When he let out a loud lion like growl, I knew he was cummin' and once he released inside of me I let go right behind him all over his dick.

"I know for a fact my son is in there. Probably even twins, ma." I ignored him as I laid there catching my breath and enjoying the moment. Kymani swore HIS son was in me each time we had sex.

"Babe, come on we have to get ready." Kymani was getting comfortable in the bed next to me and I didn't need for him to fall asleep. Yeah, I put that ass right to sleep every time. I straddled him and smiled down at him as he laid there with his eyes halfway open.

"Five minutes, E. Your little ass wore me out." His sleepy voice was even sexy. Kymani was the only person I've ever been intimate with, and I swore there was nothing else better out there for me; he always left me satisfied. My sexual appetite was for him and him only.

"When I get out the shower, Ky, you better be up," I sassed as I hopped off him and walked back into the bathroom.

In the shower, I thought about what Ky said about having his son, and I couldn't front like I didn't think about it often because I did. I just wasn't ready to be someone's mother, yet, especially with the nonexistent relationship I have with my family.

"What you in here thinking about." I thought his ass was sleeping.

"Nothing, I love you, stink."

"I love you more, E," he replied then kissed my lips. I stared into his eyes and I saw nothing but love. After we took turns washing one another up, we got out and had to rush to get dressed because Ky couldn't keep his hands to himself and we were already behind on time. This morning he told me to be ready at five and it was now going on six. Kymani picked out my clothes and I was wearing a pair of blue, ripped jeans with a pair of Margiela's and a graphic tee shirt. Of course he wanted us to match, only difference was that he wore the Future Margiela's with his Versace belt and I had on my Goyard belt. I wasn't into the social media frenzy but we looked too cute, so I snapped a few pics as we stood in the full-length mirror that was in the hallway and posted on Snapchat and Facebook.

"Ky, where are we going?" We had been driving for a minute and I didn't wanna fall asleep in the car, but I was so close to it.

"Your ass better not fall asleep, E. We'll be there in a minute." Every time Kymani took me out, it was always a surprise. I never knew where we were going until we got there, and as much as I loved surprises, I still tried to get it out of him.

When I saw the Pole Position sign ahead I instantly got excited because I had been begging Ky to take me after Cyn talked so much about it. I always complained about how he didn't listen to me when I talked, but lately he had been proving me wrong because everything my heart desired, Ky made it happen. When I wanted to go to the gun range he did that, when I wanted to try hibachi food he did that, and when I wanted to have sex on the boardwalk he did that, too.

I had the time of my life go karting even after I lost to Ky each time. I needed Cyn to teach me how to finesse the track because every time her ass walked away with the W. Cyn drove like a bat out of hell. Back in the car, Ky's phone was ringing off the hook. The number wasn't saved so I couldn't tell who it was and each time it rang he would discretely suck his teeth and act as if it wasn't bothering him, but I knew better.

"You hungry, ma?"

"Kymani, answer your phone before I do." Like I knew he would he looked at me and stared for a minute. I wasn't tripping of the call; the ringing was just irritating. I trusted Ky one hundred percent.

"Since when do I answer the phone when I'm with you, E?" He was calm as he pulled out of the parking spot and onto the highway. He was right though; not once did he answer the phone when we were out together, but usually I knew who was calling. This unknown caller had me in my feelings a little. It could be anybody.

"Here go ahead and answer it if it's bothering you that much." He tossed the phone in my lap and focused back on the road. I didn't need for him to put the passcode in or anything like that because my fingerprint was locked in his phone. I had access to his phone 24/7, so I don't know why I was tripping now. I let his phone sit in my lap after turning the ringer off and busied myself with the radio. We were having a great day and I didn't want to ruin it over some bullshit ass phone call that was probably one of his boys anyway. I sat back in my seat and felt Kymani grab ahold of my thigh as he drove. He did this whenever we were in the car together; it didn't matter who was with us. He claimed it made him feel comfortable or something like that, but Ky just couldn't keep his hands to himself. If we were near each other, he was touching me in some way shape or form. I didn't mind at all because I welcomed his touch at all times.

When we pulled up to the Red Lobster, I smiled because at first I thought he forgot what today was, but after Go Karting and now, I knew he remembered that today was the anniversary of our first date. We weren't old enough to get into Pole Position at the time without an adult, so Ky took me to Red Lobster to cheer me up. I was a seafood fanatic at the time and lived and died by Red Lobster.

"You remembered," I told him as he came around to open my door. It totally slipped my mind until we pulled up here.

"How could I forget one of the best days of my life? The day you agreed to take a nigga serious instead of just being my roommate in my granny's two-bedroom apartment was the day I vowed to do any and everything to make you the happiest girl in the world. You lost five years of your life for me. You ain't have to do the shit you did because I would've took that time, but like always you put me before everything and I could probably never repay you for that, but a nigga is going to die trying.

"For us, I did that five years for us. So that we could do exactly what we're doing now." I hated talking about my past and to me those five years didn't exist. Only thing that mattered to me was the time I spent with Kymani. I was just happy to be home.

"Now gimmie kiss, stink." Kymani bent down so that he could reach my lips as I sat halfway out the car. His kisses were always sweet and sensual I couldn't imagine myself falling for anyone else the way I fell for Ky.

We both ordered the ultimate feast and like always I was full off the biscuits and salad before our food came. I didn't have time to hear Ky clown me, so I picked at my food making it look like I was able to hang. We were in the middle of talking about where I wanted to go for vacation, like I didn't just come back from Miami, but whatever because I always wanted to go to Jamaica and I felt like that would give Ky a chance to visit his parents. Unlike me, Ky had a good relationship with his parents before they were deported back to Jamaica and I knew he missed them. So, while I was enjoying myself in a new country, he could get better acquainted with his family.

"I'm sorry about tripping over the phone earlier." For some reason, I felt the need to apologize because that wasn't like me, well us, to trip over little shit like phone calls.

"You know I wasn't worried about that shit, E." He side-eyed me as he devoured a spoonful of mashed potatoes.

"Can I get you two anything else?" the waitress asked as she stood in front of Kymani totally disregarding the fact that I was sitting there.

"The check," I firmly stated with attitude evident in my voice. Bitches were so disrespectful nowadays, I know her ass saw us sitting here together, but still she wanted to try her luck. The bitch wasn't even cute enough to sit with us.

"Will that be all?" she addressed Ky again.

"Damn, ma, you need some water or some shit cause you looking real thirsty? You heard my wife, *the check,* and that'll be all. If you walk away now she might still leave you a tip." I let Ky handle her because I knew if I was to say another word my foot would be up her ass in less than three seconds. I couldn't stand a thirsty bitch. The most she was going to get out of a nigga at the rate she was going was some hard dick and heartache and nothing more. When she came back with the check she was still salty, but the smile that was plastered on her face told me that she wanted that tip. I wasn't a spiteful bitch and I couldn't blame her for trying to get at Ky because my man was that nigga. I tossed two fifties on the table after Ky placed a hundred dollars down for our meal even though our food was no more than sixty bucks. Today was her lucky day.

Faith in my Hustla

"You're driving, ma." Ky tossed me the keys as we walked out of the restaurant. When I saw the Cold Stone sign I just had to have it; I loved ice cream.

"Please, Ky," I whined as he tried to pull me in the direction of the car. I don't know how I missed it on our way in.

"Nah, Tevin was right; your ass is really spoiled. You have a freezer full of ice-cream, E; you don't need this shit." Kymani hated Cold Stone after that time he heard that Cyn and I went with Robert and Keith one day after school. The mall used to be our hangout spot every Friday.

"I don't need it or you're still in your feelings about Robert taking me out for ice cream." I laughed as I pulled him in the direction of the store.

"That shit ain't funny, E. I almost killed your ass that night."

"Ky, it wasn't even that real. Robert was just my friend; I couldn't help the fact that he was sweet on me."

"Yeah, aiigh, get fucked up, E. I don't even know why you would bring that shit up. I don't even rock with the Timberwolves anymore ever since they drafted his ass and they used to be my favorite team."

***

"So, wassup, E, what you about to do? Me and Tee about to go O.T for a minute and I don't want your ass sitting in the house all damn day. You wanna roll with me? Your ass was always better at negotiating and shit anyway." I had been thinking about what I was going to do with myself for the past few days. I was great with numbers and helping Cyn out at the shop with the payroll and financial stuff was cool, but my dream of being a filmmaker had been eating at me as I caught up on the many webisodes that were popping right now. I could have easily taken that trip with Ky and Tevin, but I wasn't on that anymore. Kymani had shit on lock and I stepped in when needed. But I really wanted to go to school to get a taste of a little bit of everything. Being locked up at seventeen offered me the opportunity to connect with a lot of young people who were just like me or worse off than me. Their families didn't give a shit about them and they were forced into the streets. Whereas I had a choice, they didn't. I wanted to start a youth program that helped me reach them before they did whatever it was that'll land them in jail. It would more or less be like a big sister program catering to boys and girls from the ages of fourteen to seventeen. I had a plan, and with Ky away for a few weeks, I planned on taking that step to get it started. Alana and Cyn both had stayed up with me countless nights on conference calls helping me sort out my ideas. Kymani didn't care what I did one way or the other, he just wanted to keep spoiling me.

"I enrolled in school a few weeks back. The semester starts next week," I nervously said because I never had the school conversation with Ky. It was always Cyn and Alana listening to me vent about my dreams. I knew Kymani would support me one hundred and ten percent I was just nervous to tell him because college was never in our plans. I barely wanted to graduate high school even with a 4.0 GPA.

"School? Stop playing, E. I don't want you sitting in the house getting fat and shit." I flipped him off and sat up from the seat I was laid out on in the movie room.

"I'm serious, Ky. Look." I showed him the conformation email.

"Oh, shit, you were dead ass." Kymani grabbed me up and lifted me in his arms like I was a child. I hated that I was so small because Ky took that to heart and did whatever with me. I was always in his arms or on his back. He showered my face with kisses while he spun around with me still in his arms.

"Ky, stop; I'm dizzy."

"Real shit, I'm proud of you, ma. I knew your geeky ass was up to something when I saw you in those books."

"Thank you, stink. So, go handle your business; I'll be fine I promise. I even got Cyn to enroll part-time with me. If you need me, just call me." I told him once he placed me back on my feet. Cyn wasn't hell bent on school, but since I asked I knew she wasn't going to tell me no. She low-key wanted to go too, she just didn't want to admit it. Alana already had her Bachelor's degree and was doing her Master's online. The way she handled her business is what Cyn and I hoped to embody

"Aiigh, I'm going to call you as soon as we land. I love you, stink."

"No, you're my, stink. I love you more. Miss one FaceTime or text and I'm on the first flight don't fuck with me, Kymani." I was dead ass serious and he knew it. Me and Cyn already let them know what it was.

"Just make sure y'all behave for a nigga." I waved him off because with Cyn anything was possible.

"I got about five minutes before Tee gets here. You gon' take care of ya man?"

"Five minutes, Ky? That's a tease, hell no." I was just playing with him; I would never deny my baby. Plus, I didn't know when he was coming back so our daily sessions were going to be nonexistent.

"Man, you don't even have to do anything," he whined.

"And I'm the spoiled one." I laughed as I pulled him towards the door. My theater room was sacred and a no sex zone; the guest bedroom across the hall would have to do.

Chapter Six

Kymani

Tevin was the wrong nigga to go O.T with when you were in a relationship. Now that E was home there was certain shit I couldn't do that I used to enjoy when we traveled out of town. Big booty stripper bitches being at the top of the list. If it was a year ago and I only had Lia to worry about, then I would be all for it, but I wasn't about to disrespect E like that. Tevin, on the other hand, his ass ain't care. Plus, Cyn ain't bless him before he left so my boy was running down on everything moving in the strip club. I let his ass know he could look but not touch. I wasn't about to be held responsible for him fucking up again. Nah, not after he just got his girl back; my boy couldn't go out like that. Hell, if it wasn't for this nigga, Drayco, I wouldn't even be here, but out of respect for my man and the way he did business I was sitting back and enjoying the atmosphere. I knew my limits, and whenever we went out E always let a nigga do him as long as I kept it PG, but there was nothing PG about these down south broads, that's why Tevin liked coming out here.

Drayco was our pill and weed connect that E had set us up with through one of her home girls in the pen. This nigga had that good shit too. I ain't fuck with no pills but his weed always gave a nigga that good high. Not that fake ass loud that niggas were pushing in the hood. Now that I thought about it, my baby deserved a new gift because everything that she brought to the table was A1. Drayco was cool as hell for a white boy, and the way he carried himself I sometimes forgot it was a white boy I was chilling wit'. I fucked with Dray because he ain't try to fit in. He moved at his own beat and niggas knew not to fuck with him. They ain't call his ass Drayco just because; my boy was real right out here in The Bay. Every time we touched down, Drayco showed us a good time. It was always business first and once that was over everything was a go.

"I heard your lady is home. My sister was geeked as fuck when she heard she was out. I was kind of hoping you brought her down with you so she could get off my back." Brittney was probably the only person E spoke to on some real shit while she was in there. Other than that, she claimed them broads wasn't real right. Brittney was released a year before E and I could have easily gotten her number from Drayco or vice versa, but we had a rule that we didn't contact one another unless it was business related.

"Maybe when you finally bring your ass out to New York, Britt could slide through, too. I know E would be happy to see her."

"Sounds like a plan, bro." I didn't 'bro' a lot of niggas, but Drayco was my man a hunned grand and we broke bread together. He had earned that title a while ago. Him and Tevin were the only two niggas I tolerated that bro shit from; I was Money to everyone else. Me and my team were about to come up something crazy because the pills and weed moved itself. As much shit as white America talked, it was their kids that I made most of my money off of when it came to moving them pills. They partied hard as fuck off them shits while we stuck to what we knew and that was some good herb and some spirits. I wasn't about that pill life at all. The way money was coming in, I would be able to retire in a few years, but until then I was gon' grind harder than I ever did to make sure E and Azia don't want for nothing. They were my main priorities; everything else after them was irrelevant. As long as my family was good, I was straight. With Cyn and E's shop doing so well, I was looking to open a barbershop or two and even a lounge, so when I walked away my shit would be solid.

Faith in my Hustla

When E came home, I ain't expect her to fall back into the day to day shit because before she went in, it was her that held shit down. I just followed her lead and now that she was talking that school shit, it just solidified the plans I had for us. I was gon' seed her up with the rest of my kids and let her do her thing while I ran the streets and took care of my business with my niggas. Lia really was a mistake and I knew sooner or later her ass was gon' become a pain in my ass, but for now I was enjoying the peace and quiet as long as I kept her ass laced in Gucci and Louie. Whether it was FaceTime or pop-up visits, I made sure Azia heard my voice and saw my face every day. Azia may not have been planned, but I didn't love my princess any less because she didn't ask to be here and I loved being her father. My pops may not have been in my life full time, but he was there and there isn't a bad memory that I have of him from my childhood. I wanted to give Azia that times ten; my princess deserved everything the world had to offer.

YFN Lucci played through the speakers and I rapped along to the words as everybody got amped off the lyrics. Lucci was that nigga and street niggas could relate to what he was spitting. That's why half the club was going word for word to his "Documentary" track. Tevin had some big booty chick giving him a lap dance while he tossed hundreds and fifties over her. We never came to the club with anything less than twenties and it was rare that you caught us with dubs. That's why the stripper chicks loved us because before the night was over, me and my niggas were sure to pay off car notes, rent, tuition, all that shit. I sat back facing a bottle of Ace of Spades and thought about calling E, but I knew she wouldn't be able to hear me over this noise, and I ain't need my boys clowning me because I dipped off to the car to call wifey. I was chilling and once I lit this fat ass blunt I was going to be zooted for sure. E was all the woman I needed and I wouldn't dare slip up with a stripper. No disrespect to them, but I wasn't going out like that. Sanaa Lathan and Regina King both would be having to throw it at a nigga at the same damn time for me to fuck around on E. I've fucked around with a few chicks in my time and still after all these years not a female compared to my baby. She was the only person that could put my ass to sleep. Real shit though, as much as she admired Sanaa, I don't even think she would mind even then. Taraji and Sanaa were Erin's all time favs and I know they had a lot to do with her wanting to take up film, aside from her love for movies. There wasn't a nigga alive that I saw competing with me for E's heart because as soon as the nigga showed face, it was lights out for his ass. The only reason that scrub, Robert, lived to see another day was because he was the hood's favorite and people would have noticed when he was gone. So I let his ass live his nice lil' life as long as he stayed away from what was mine. I wasn't no insecure nigga by far, but for E, I'd run down on any and everything without even thinking twice.

There was a trio in front of me, bouncing their ass all up in a nigga grill. They were so in sync with one another that I was getting dizzy. As big as their asses were, it still wasn't enough for me to touch. The sight was amazing, though, and I made sure to toss the bills freely from the stack of money that was sitting on the table in front of me.

"Yo, my nigga, that's my bitch." Was the last thing I heard before shots rang out. I looked to my left to make sure my niggas were straight and of course it was Tevin's ass the big, brolic nigga was talking to. My brother's shits worked so I wasn't worried about him holding his own, but the shots turned shit all the way up. I pushed the three chicks behind me and did my best to shield them as I pulled my piece just as the nigga was pouring his heart out to Tee. And that right there is where he fucked up because everybody, well almost everybody, knew not to pull out unless they were really about that life. Without hesitation, I started firing at that nigga making sure to hit him in places that weren't too detrimental to his livelihood, no chick was worth losing his life over. If my nigga wanted him dead after I laid his ass down, then it was what it was. It'll be one less bitch nigga we had in this world. The nigga, Drayco, was giving his partner the business as Tevin stood over ol' boy with a wicked ass grin on his face. There was a bunch of people around so I knew today was this nigga's lucky day because Tevin was ready to end this nigga's career.

"Yo, bro, we off this." I pulled Drayco off his mans and we made our way to the back exit, leaving everyone in the midst of chaos. Dray was a petty nigga so he had to get one last kick before he caught up to us. I was glad we weren't fifty deep in the spot because this scene could've turned out way worse.

"My nigga, Money, saves the day again." Drayco laughed as we hopped in the rental I copped once we touched down.

"Yeah with his super save a hoe ass. On the town, I was gon' end that fool," Tevin slurred and I couldn't help but to laugh because his ass was too busy into the nigga's girl to even see him pop up, and his ass was gon' catch his fade if I ain't step in when I did.

"I need to eat before I head back to the hotel. That hotel food don't be hitting like it used to. E got my ass spoiled; I hate eating out now."

"You's a lucky boy. I wish I had that. All I know is take out and drive-thrus. Brittney's ass don't be trying to feed me. She claims I'm too old to not know how to cook and shit. It's a diner right across from the hotel. We could go there, and I'll have somebody come scoop me after we eat."

"Say that, bro." I pulled off in the direction of the hotel, and once we sat down I checked my phone and saw that E had text me. I was doing good with not missing calls and text messages, so I hurriedly replied before she started her shit.

"Ol' in love ass nigga. This nigga got two bitches back at home. Lucky ass nigga." Tevin had the nerve and if looks could kill his ass would be six feet under maybe twelve 'cause Dray had the same facial expression as me. It was becoming a habit of his to speak on my situation with Lia and Erin, and again I was questioning his life because, yet again, he was throwing shade like a bitch. What if I was on the phone with E and he said some fly shit like that?

"You's a wild boy," Drayco said once our food arrived and Tee just shrugged him off. The sad part about the shit was that he didn't find anything wrong with what he was saying. Again, I ignored his ass like I did the last few times and chalked it up to him being drunk and tore into my food. Dray said that their steak and shrimp was aiigh, so that's what I fucked with and it wasn't half bad. Hell, it was on hunned for a nigga that was on E.

"My ride is here. I'm gonna holla at you on the wake up before y'all dip, bro. Aye, Tee, hold ya head like it, lil' bro." I dapped Dray up and finished off my food to head up to my room and call my baby. Tevin could sit down there all he wanted. I was cool on his shady ass for now. I paid the bill and left a tip because, if it was up to Tee, waiters didn't deserve tips because they were just doing their jobs.

"Hey, stink," Erin sheepishly answered the FaceTime with a smile. Seeing her face had me forgetting about all the bullshit that had just transpired. I stripped out of my street clothes and chopped it up with my heart. E was laying in the bed with the T.V on but the volume was off as usual. I low-key thought she feared the dark because she couldn't sleep in complete darkness. Even if I came in after her and turned the T.V off, she'd wake up and turn the shit right back on.

"I'm surprised your other half isn't all up in the camera," I joked because Cyn had been over the house almost every day since we left. If she wasn't over there, E was at her crib. I shook my head when E flipped the camera and I saw Cyn knocked out in our bed like she didn't have a care in the world. We talked a little more before E ended up falling asleep on me. She started classes a few days ago and my baby was tired. Usually it was me that fell asleep first; I placed the phone down on the pillow and made sure not to hang up and went to handle my hygiene. I didn't have time to hear her mouth in the morning about me hanging up, so I let her rock because had she hung up on me I would have got in her ass.

***

"Fuck, man." Tee had been yelling out obscenities since we got in the car and I had been ignoring his ass, but now he was just doing it to get my attention.

"Fuck wrong with you?" I laughed as he hung his head low and slouched in the passenger seat. We were on our way to check with Drayco to make sure everything was everything before we headed back home.

"Nothing, my nigga. I don't know why you even going to check with this nigga. We got everything we needed; fuck we still out here for?" I swear Tevin had been on some real bitch shit lately from dropping Lia comments and whining all fucking day. Drayco was cool as hell and I couldn't understand for the life of me why Tee constantly threw him shade.

"You's a shady nigga, yo. Why you always in ya damn feelings, bro, like a bitch? Dray breaks bread with us freely and never came at us with no bullshit, but yet you acting like he did something to you."

"I just don't like his ass. He swears he knows you and shit. All that bro shit; that's E peoples; not yours," Tee barked. Who was this nigga? I was going to check Cyn and see if her ass was pregnant or some shit because lately Tee had been in his bag. I ain't know how much more of this shit I could take, so I turned the music up and let his ass sit in his feelings.

When we pulled up to Drayco's crib, Tee took his time getting out, dragging his feet like a small child that couldn't get their way. I knew Dray saw the shit but he wasn't worried about Tevin's ass.

"What's good, B?" I acknowledged Britt as I made my way through the backyard. There were a few people from Dray's camp out along with Britt's friends. Brittney was about five-foot-six, just a little taller than E, and she was tatted up something crazy. Her whole demeanor reminded me of E and it was crazy because her mouth was just as reckless. The way she held Drayco down was A1. The two of them had The Bay on lock.

"Hey, Money, how's my girl?" she asked and I could see she was genuinely concerned about E.

"She's good, great actually with her spoiled ass. When Dray comes to New York, you should pull up; I know she'd love to see you."

"Andrew's ass ain't going to New York, but I'll definitely come check my girl." B was always dissing Drayco. The fact that he was a major hitter meant nothing to her; he'll always be little Andrew to her.

"Say that, I just came to show face before I dipped out. Here this her calling now." I passed Britt the phone and covered my ears from all the screaming her and E were doing. I wasn't in a rush, so I let them chop it up while I grabbed something to eat. They had the grill out and were throwing down.

"What's good with your boy?" Drayco asked me once I sat down with my plate. I didn't even know how to answer his ass because Tee was my blood and no matter how much of a bitch he was being I wasn't gon' downplay him to the next man.

"He good, bro; don't pay his moody ass no mind." Drayco just nodded his head and if Tee couldn't stay out his feeling I was going to start making these trips doley. Now that E was focusing on school, I wasn't even going to bother asking her.

Once I touched down, I hit my man Esco and had him handle the drop offs for today since Tee was still in his feeling and I had to go check my favorite girl.

When I pulled into the driveway of Lia's spot, I could hear Azia yelling from the doorway as she jumped up and down. "Daddy, daddy!" she screamed as I hopped out and made my way to the front door. Azia was running towards me at full speed.

"Slow down, A." Baby girl was growing by the second. She seemed a little taller from the last time I saw her.

"Daddy, I missed you."

"I missed you more, A. what you been up too?" I picked her up and tossed her up in the air a little while she laughed.

"Mommy brought me new dolls and a car. You wanna see my car, daddy. It's pink." A week ago, I had my man hook her up with an pink Benz just like the one I got E.

Lia's ass ain't buy shit, but I wasn't petty so I didn't blow her up. I sat down on the couch with Azia still in my arms as she showered my face with kisses. Lia stood by the door with the meanest grill but I didn't come over here to rap with her I came to chill with my daughter. Azia was my heart and I'd never start some shit with her mom's in front of her. Lia was drop dead gorgeous and when I met her she was a full-time model. Now she took a few jobs here and there because she felt like it. She didn't know how much I was banking, so she felt like she needed to model to keep some extra cash around. I had mad love for Lia, but we could never be because I didn't love her. I just respected her as the mother of my child, but she wanted more from a nigga that I couldn't offer her. So I tried to keep her ass satisfied with the finer things but all she wanted was the d and since E been home, I cut her ass off completely.

"A, you weren't giving mommy a hard time, right?" Azia always turned up when she couldn't get her way with Lia and it was always 'Kymani talk to your daughter.' I had her little ass spoiled rotten, but my princess deserved the world. She was starting school soon, so I was trying to fall back a little. I didn't need her turning up in school.

"I was a good girl, Daddy. Look I can write you and Mommy's name now." Azia hopped off my lap and went to grab her notebook and pencil from the kitchen table. When she came back, she sat down at the end table and started my name first. I was surprised when she wrote out Kymani instead of Daddy.

"Mommy taught me how to spell your name see K-y-m-a-n-i." Lia emerged from the back with a plate of food and a cup of lemonade in hand. Lia couldn't cook worth shit, so I hired a chef to come and help her prepare meals. There was no way she was going to raise my daughter and not know how to cook. She couldn't burn like my baby, but Lia had improved in the kitchen so I wasn't as hesitant as I usually was to accept a plate of food from her. I looked at Lia's light skin complexion and saw how that was the only thing that Azia inherited from her. She still wore her hair in a silk press and her hazel eyes shined a little if she stood in the sun or in any light. I smiled at her because she was beautiful and there was no denying that.

"What? Why are you looking at me like that, Kymani?" She sat across from me on the couch while Azia busied herself doodling on the sheet pf paper. I knew there was something that she wanted to get off her chest but was afraid to.

"Wassup, Li, what's on your mind? I asked as I dug into the spaghetti she had prepared.

"Nothing. I'm good; you made it clear that you don't wanna be with me and I know there's probably a hundred bitches entertaining you." Azia spun her head around so fast after she heard Lia curse, and I almost spit my food out as she scolded her.

"Mommy, Daddy says you can't use bad words or you'll go in time out. Now say sorry." She stood there with her hands on her hips and waited for her mother to apologize.

"I'm sorry, baby."

"A, come give daddy kiss I'm going to see you later, okay." I kissed Azia on her forehead and stood to leave. There was no way I was having this conversation in front of my daughter. Lia's ass was spoiled too. I really had to get my shit together and boss up. All the woman in my life were spoiled as hell.

"I love you, Daddy," Azia sadly said and I wanted so badly to take her with me.

"Fifteen fucking minutes, Kymani. That's all we're worth; fifteen minutes," Lia yelled as she followed me to my car. I didn't hit females at all, but I was about three seconds from beating a bitches' ass if she put her hands on me again.

"Lia, go ahead with that shit you really on some bullshit. I came to see my daughter, not argue with your ass."

"Why can't we come with you? Why can't we get one night?

Chapter Seven

Tevin

Five years ago, when E got pinched I thought our whole operation was done because her ass was the brains behind everything. While CK was molding Money into the man he wanted him to be, Alana was doing the same with E. It was like just fuck Tee; he'd figure it out on his own and it's been like that since I was a youngin' robbing and killing niggas just because. Nobody ever showed me anything. I learned all that shit on my own: how to trap, get money, rob, and kill all me. Tevin Marquis Daniels is a self-made nigga and this nigga, Money, was just a come-up. I didn't kill him because he proved to be beneficial. On the real, Drayco's days were numbered because I felt like he was gunning for my spot as Money's right hand man and I couldn't have that. Money was my nigga but I didn't understand the need for extra niggas when he had me a motherfucker that could do it all. Drayco was our supplier and nothing more. All that bro shit irritated the fuck out of me. When I was a youth, the teachers and guidance counselors used to say I had a possessive complex or some shit like that. But I wasn't trying to hear that shit, I just wanted what I wanted when I wanted it and not nan motherfucker could tell me otherwise.

I watched as Money and Dray chopped it up and how they kept side-eyeing a nigga every other minute, but I was cool on them. He could say what he wanted as long as he didn't step to me on no bullshit I was straight. I wasn't really focused on their little conversation because I was thinking of a way to execute my plan. My boy, Ahmad, that I grew up with back in the day was fresh home and looking for a come up and I had just the plan for him. Ahmad and I used to hit all the big trap houses and split everything down the middle and I knew it would be like stealing candy from a baby since I knew the ins and outs of Money's operation. Everybody thought that this was our shit, but on the real everything moved through E and Money and I was just a replacement while E was gone. I knew once Money got hold of the hit he'd flip the script and want to move everything around, and I'd finally be able to know where he kept his stash house. On top of that, once niggas started selling his shit on blocks that we didn't control I knew some shit was sure to pop off. I was looking to start a full-blown street war.

"Yo, we out, kid," Money said after he dapped Drayco up and hugged Brittney. I threw his ass a head nod and made my way to the truck with my plate of food. I may not have fucked with ole boy, but his sister threw down something serious on the grill. When we got in the car, Money was cracking up but I ain't see shit funny. The ride to the airport was short so I didn't even try to get comfortable. Plus, the way his ass drove the GPS said twenty, Money was getting us there in nine flat. I sent Cyn a text so that she could meet me at the airport, I wasn't trying to parlay another minute. I missed my baby girl and Money drove us to the airport, so that meant I would have had to do drop offs with him when we touched down and I wasn't with it.

The eight-hour flight had me drowsy and hungrier than I was when I boarded. That plate I grabbed did nothing but hold me over for an hour, maybe two. Cyn wasn't big on cooking. She was take out queen and I hoped like hell she was in the mood to whip me up something to eat. I didn't feel like eating out today. It was the middle of the day and her ass didn't have class or anything else to do but hair; she had time to feed a nigga.

As me and Money walked through LaGuardia, bitches were gawking hard as hell and everything in me wanted to run down, but Cyn was close by and I didn't have time for no bullshit especially not with Mr. Faithful with me. Ever since E touched down, this nigga didn't even look at a chick too long. I used to be able to run down on any and everything with my boy. Now his ass was so far up E's ass, that the chicks just started falling back.

"Hey, Pa," Cyn sexily said as she stood in front of her Benz like the boss ass chick that she was.

"Wassup, sis."

"Hey, Money." They hugged briefly and Money headed to the parking lot where his car was.

"I missed you, ma." I pulled Cyn in for a hug while I playfully grabbed a handful of her ass.

"I missed you more. I made your favorite at my place." I side-eyed her because I had left her at my spot and there was no reason for her to go back to her apartment.

"Don't look at me like that, Marquis. I had class and appointments that I couldn't do at the shop, so I had them come to my house. Plus, your house is too big for me to be there all by myself.

"But you could sit up in E and Money shit all day with no problem. Man, go ahead with that shit," I spat as I opened the door for her to get in then made my way around to the passenger side.

"Yeah, let me get you fed because nobody has time for that nasty ass attitude. I have a test in the morning for my Psychology 101 class and I need to study."

"Yeah after you take this dick you can do whatever you please, ma." She rolled her eyes, but I was dead ass serious. I've been gone for a whole two weeks and some change; I needed some lay up tonight. I hooked my phone up to the Bluetooth and turned off Cyn's sad ass love songs. I fucked with Mary J hard but not right now. My boy, G Herbo, had just dropped some new shit and I hadn't gotten around to blessing my life yet. That new Meek Mill x Lil Bibby and PNB Rock went hard too. I made sure to play that because Cyn liked the song. We rapped along to the lyrics as we made our way back to Brooklyn to Cyn's spot.

"Shoes please." Every time I pulled up over here I had to discard myself of my shoes and outerwear. Cyn was a real neat freak and low key germaphobe. I couldn't sit on her bed in my street clothes, but her and E stayed in the shit fully clothed and shit. The smell of fried chicken had my stomach talking back, so I hurriedly removed my shoes and made my way to the sink as Cyn busied herself in the kitchen making our plates. I checked the refrigerator for something to drink and was happy as hell when I saw the two Peach

Orchard Minute Maids in the fridge because Cyn drunk a whole bunch of expensive shit that I couldn't even pronounce. She acted like she was too good for Kool Aid and Minute Maid juices by the gallon.

"Good looking, bae." Fried chicken and Baked Ziti were my favorite dishes and Cyn had made both with a side of cheesy garlic bread.

"You're welcome," she said as she kissed my forehead and sat across from me as we ate and talked briefly about my trip. Cyn wasn't a dummy. She knew what I was into, she just didn't know as much as E and that's how I planned on keeping it. If shit went down, I didn't want her to have to go down for my bullshit; the less she knew the better. Cyn was the only peace I had in my life. When I was with her, she made a nigga feel normal and needed. I didn't have to be the thugged out street nigga with her, and my money and status didn't faze her. She fucked with me the long way and I was going to try my best and do right by her this time around. I had some shit cooking up and if Cyn played her cards right she was gon' be straight forever. First, I had to handle Niecy's conniving ass, she had been blowing me up something crazy with this whole baby shit.

***

On the way over to the hospital, I thought about everything Cyn had said to me and the plans we had just made moving forward. Cyn was my heart and there was no denying that if that baby turned out to be mine I knew for a fact she'd leave a nigga after all that shit I spat about not fucking around with Niecy. The nurse at the front desk was bad as hell and if I was on a different type of time I would've chopped it up with her ass, but I was in enough shit as is. I kept it pushing to the room Niecy had texted me and said a silent prayer to keep me cool. Shaniece had the ability to bring out the worst in a nigga, her mouth was something crazy and she didn't give a fuck either.

Opening the door to room 402 I watched as she laid there sleepily with the baby in her arms. All I needed was to get a full look at the baby because my smoke grey eyes and dirty brown hair with a hint of red was something that didn't go unnoticed. Her home girl Amanda was standing over them complimenting the baby's good looks in between eye fucking me.

"He looks just like his daddy, sis." Amanda wanted to smash a nigga bad so she would come and get in my ear about Niecy then end up with a nigga's dick in her mouth. She was foul as fuck and the look she gave me after the statement she made told me this baby wasn't mine. I stood there a while waiting for Niecy to acknowledge me, but she didn't; she kept her eyes trained on the baby.

"You called me down here for a baby with blue eyes and blonde hair. Bitch, I should kill you just off GP." I couldn't hold back my laughter because she was salty as hell. I know she hoped and prayed that baby came out at least favoring me in some way, but he looked nothing like me and everything like the old, white cat she was fucking around with since high school. Me and Niecy went way back, before Cyn there was Shaniece. I fucked with her the long way and my young ass was whipped by that upper classmen box and the way Niecy put it down in the bedroom was enough to keep me in line. She had that 'I'd kill any motherfucker for looking her way box,' but her hood rat ways were what I couldn't put up with. She lived for nights in the trap with my crew and making drug runs and shit. In the beginning, it was all cool because I had a down ass bitch, but when I leveled up she was supposed to as well, but that shit never happened. Niecy lived for that hood fame and not the fame like E and Alana had, that's what I couldn't fuck with. I needed a lady, not a homie. When I got up with Cyn, I realized how much I was playing myself fucking with her. As a boss I needed a boss ass bitch.

"You just have to give him time to grow into his features, Tee. He's only a day old. My great-grandmother is white; that's probably why he has the features. Nah, she wasn't dead ass; Ms. Jones was as black as they came, no disrespect intended.

"Yo, Niecy, hit me up and maybe I'll buy him some Jays and some pampers. That's the best I can do for you because I know your situation. A, hold your head like it hurt, ma." I tossed a few bills at the foot of her bed and made my exit. I couldn't front; I was relieved as fuck because a few times we did mess around I ran up in her raw doggy like the careless nigga I was. Most times Niecy and I hooked up, I was either high as hell or tore up off that dirty.

"Tevin!" I heard her shouting but the proof was in her hands and the fact that she was too blind to see it worried me. I ain't need no baby mama drama like that nigga Money was sure to have. He couldn't keep E a secret from Lia forever. They were going to cross paths eventually and I couldn't wait until they did. I couldn't stand Lia's uppity ass no way. I breathed a sigh of relief once I hit the elevator, thanking the man upstairs for sparing me the bullshit that was to come if Niecy was my baby mother.

"So, when am I going to see you again," Amanda's thot ass said once I stepped into the elevator I didn't even know she was behind me. Her best friend was in the same room we both had just left out of, crying over the same dick she was so desperately trying to get a taste of. Amanda was all in my personal space trying to get a reaction out of me as her breast rubbed up against my chest. Her breathing sped up as I closed that small gap between us and towered over her. I ain't really fuck with itty bitty chicks, but A was bad. The look in her eyes told me that I could have my way with her right here in this elevator if I wanted to.

"A, on the real, I'm cool on you. Me and my lady trying to work some shit out and I know she wouldn't appreciate you coming at me like this." I knew mentioning Cyn as my lady would put her in a sour mood because she worked at the same shop Cyn and E ran. Yeah, this shit was crazy. Amanda wasn't stupid so I wasn't worried about her mentioning this shit to Cyn. I'd be at her head so fast like she was a nigga in the streets. Cyn was every hood nigga's dream and I wasn't trying to fuck that up this time around. I could have easily taken A in one of these rooms and blew her back out, but I knew that shit would crush Cyn and she was the only person I cared for on some real shit. I was trying to keep my dick in my pants and out these bitches. A few months ago, you probably couldn't pay me to be tied down to one female, but I knew if I didn't get my shit together I would lose Cyn forever.

"Yeah, bae." I answered the phone while Amanda stood there with an attitude, but not my bitch, not my problem. It would be just my luck Cyn called me when I was out here doing some shit I had no business doing. The elevators doors opened and I left Amanda's big mad ass standing there. Cyn was telling me how her test went and I was proud that she aced the shit. My baby was really taking this school flex serious. E really had the ability to level up your life up. She did it with Money, me, and now Cyn.

"I'm going to have to get you a gift for acing your first test, huh." The small laugh on the other end of the phone confirmed that she was expecting a gift. She had been asking for another Pandora bracelet and I was probably going to get her that. Cyn loved simple ass gifts and that's why I always went above and beyond for her when it was time for gifts. She hadn't gotten a bag out of me in a minute and she was long overdue for one. I watched as Amanda walked past my car with an extra step in her walk and my dick jumped a little because A had ass for days. She was super thick in all the right places and she wasn't bad on the eyes either. If she wasn't such an eater, she could have easily been wifed up, but she chose to live the life of rat. The best part about having eyes was that just because I couldn't touch didn't mean I couldn't look, especially if the site was giving me Delicious from the *Flava of Love* vibes.

"Aiigh, bae, I'm gonna hit you when I get to the hood. I just got in the car. I love you more." I was on my way to the hood. Money had called me a while ago saying some shit had went down. When I pulled up to the warehouse, I saw a few familiar cars and knew this shit had to be important if everyone was out.

"I'm going to give y'all niggas one last time to come clean. I'm gone for a week and y'all motherfuckers act like shit is sweet. That's 25k unaccounted for. Where the fuck is my bread?" Money barked as he had four little niggas on their knees in front of our whole camp. I was surprised to see Money in action because I thought his ass had went soft on me ever since his girl came home. He was preaching that peace and prosperity shit that E was talking, but this was the

Money I knew in the flesh, ruthless as fuck. I'm guessing they thought because Money was always the calmer and level headed one that he was the one to fuck with, but somebody should've told their asses better.

"Man, I don't know what you're talking about. I ain't have anything to do with this." One of the young boys cried out. They were all bloody and looked like they caught these hands.

"Aiigh, say that, so since your ass is so innocent tell me who the fuck had something to do with it. Last I checked, the four of you were in charge of the trap over in the east and I'm short twenty-five bands, so somebody better get to talking or it's lights out for all four of y'all asses." The youngin' looked over to his mans with pleading eyes and automatically Money knew who was the ring leader. He walked over to the table that sat in the middle of the room and removed his T-shirt. Money was the only dude I knew that still wore wife beaters as undershirts with his ole proper ass. When he wrapped his hands, I knew he was about to give these niggas the business. On the real, Money's hands were nothing to fuck with and were his biggest weapon. He'd beat your ass before he picked up a gun or any other weapon.

141

WHAP! WHAP!

Money sent a killer two piece to Dre, the one we assumed to be the ring leader, and had his ass dazed. Then went on to deliver the same blows to the other three repeatedly. If they were smart they would've jumped his ass being that none of them were tied up or anything like that. I knew for a fact if somebody was wailing me and my boys out like that we would have rushed his ass. These little niggas ain't know no better and they stole from the wrong nigga.

"Man, Dre, speak the fuck up! I told you not to do this shit; now you all mute and shit." Chris shouted through bloody lips. Still Dre said nothing and Chris went on to tell everyone his plan.

"Real shit, Money. I ain't know until you brought this shit up today and Dre's punk ass had been talking about skipping town with Lee and Jet once they hit a lick. Had I known he was talking about you, I would've took care of the shit myself. But I ain't know and now we're here, so just get this shit over. I'm not about to keep getting beat on for the next man's bullshit." These dudes were getting paid good money to sit on their ass and keep shit under control, and they had the nerve to bite the hands that fed them. I knew after Chris's lil' spiel, Money wasn't going to harm him anymore because he respected him for standing up for himself while his buddies let him get caught up in some shit that had nothing to do with him. Chris looked hella familiar, but I couldn't pinpoint who it was that he resembled. When I brought it up to Money, his ass ain't know either, but we both agreed that his face was real familiar. Chris was about seventeen and had been working for us for a few months. He just moved out here from Chicago with his moms.

"25k, though, y'all little niggas willing to die over twenty-five bands. I respect you for keeping it tall with me." Money shook his head after he dapped a bloody Chris up and grabbed his nine from his waist. The room grew extra silent, anticipating what was to come next. Almost everyone in this room had either taken a life or saw someone take a life, but still the shit wasn't something you looked forward to seeing. When Money raised his nine to Dre's head and pulled the trigger, his shit split instantly and Lee and Jet both looked scared straight, but it was too late. There was no way Money was letting them live. He walked over to Chris and handed him the piece. No words needed to be spoken; he knew what had to be done.

BOC! BOC! BOC! BOC!

He sent two to each of their chests and watched as they took their last breaths before sending one to each of their heads. This little nigga was about that gun play. He didn't even flinch when he pulled the trigger and looked down at the three lifeless bodies before him that were his homies. I knew that shit fucked him up, but he was doing a hell of a job not showing it.

Money dismissed himself as he made his way to the back room probably to clean himself up.

"Aiigh, clean this shit up. These niggas don't deserve no funeral," I stated as I sat down at the table with a few of my niggas and lit one in the air. I had some time to spare before I made it home to Cyn. So I was going to chill with my mans for a few before I dipped off. Money came back and sat at the head of the table and poured himself a glass of Henny. I wanted to ease the mood, so I lit everyone up with that fye and offered them a drink. Today was supposed to be the day the youngin's spit for me and Money for the grand prize of 5gs. There was three rounds and Cam that went by Killer and Will that went by Willz were the ones that made it to the finals and since they were here Money figured why not let them spit right now. Both of them went hard, so I knew this was going to be hard round to judge but there could only be one winner, even though Money and I were both putting up 5gs so that they could invest in their craft with some studio time or whatever they chose to do.

"Aiigh, I'm about to get out of here. I promised Lia that I'd take her and A out tonight. Might hit up Outback. A loves their coconut shrimp.

"Tell my god baby I said wassup, A Money." I dapped Money up after he handed me the five bands.

Chapter Eight

Erin

When I woke up I've never been so excited for a Wednesday in my life, but Wednesday was me and Cyn's new Friday   and I was looking forward to my weekend of no work. I handed in all my assignments for the week early, so that I didn't have to worry about missing deadlines. Cyn and I were using this weekend to study for our upcoming Psych 101 test. I was running a little late and Cyn was blowing me up. Plus, Ky let me sleep through all three of my alarms this morning. I hurriedly slipped on my jeans and grabbed the closest pair of sneakers after pulling my Iron Madden t-shirt over my head. I kissed a sleeping Kymani goodbye and of course his ass wanted to wake up when I was on my way out the door.

"Have a good day, ma." I heard him say as I rushed down the stairs and out the door to Cyn's impatient ass.

"Good morning, sissy." I sang as I fastened my seatbelt. Not because it was the law but because Cynthia had no business behind the wheel of a car. I always said a silent prayer before we pulled off.

"Morning, bihh. If Professor Noel starts that 'Ladies, Ladies you're late if you're on time' bullshit today I'm going to kick your ass, man," Cyn whined as she pulled out of my driveway.

"We're only a few minutes behind schedule we'll make it."

"Here I got you breakfast; no swine for your Allah Hu Akbar ass." Cyn and Ky found my new religion a joke but as the days went by both of them had cut out swine from their diets and had been practicing the teachings of the Quran. Every day I prayed Cyn was right beside me and every night I caught Ky saying "Amin" after he said his prayers as well.

When Cyn pulled into our shared parking spot, it was 9:05 and we had more than enough time to make it to class, Brooklyn College was big but not that big once you got used to it. Majority of our classes were in the same building. Every day I sat down in my seat in the second row near the window. It felt like my first day all over again as we waited for Professor Noel to grace us with her presence. I had my Mac Book out that Cyn had custom made for me in pink and I did hers in purple. I opened the Psychology 101 notes tab and reread a few things just in case she came in here asking questions from the readings. Once Professor Noel made her grand entrance like the diva she was, she immediately began to lecture and the room that was once filled with chatter fell silent. We went over what was expected for us on Monday's exam and as always Cynthia had a million and one questions. Cyn was so attentive and never missed a beat, while I remembered what was most important; I left the miscellaneous stuff to her. Professor Noel lectured for about thirty minutes asking questions in-between and like every class she left the last ten minutes of class for open discussion. While majority of the class quickly dispersed a few of us stayed behind making sure we had what we needed for the exam. Tuition was way too high for us to play with our education.

The rest of our day was a blur as we sat through two more lectures and study hall, finally leaving campus around five thirty. I hadn't heard from Kymani since this morning and he told me last night that he was going to be running the streets all day, so I sent him a text just checking in and didn't trip when he didn't respond right away like he usually did. Cyn and I had hooked up with two students from our class who had the same vison as us and were just as serious about making a difference in our communities. Tyquan and Yancy were only nineteen, but they were just the kids I was looking to connect with because they were more connected with the youth and community than I was. Yancy was born and raised in Far Rockaway while Tyquan was from Forty Projects in south side Jamaica Queens. They had met in high school in eleventh grade and had been inseparable since.

"Sis, your brother just texted me and asked can I pick him up some coconut shrimp from Outback. You want me to drop you off first or you're riding with me?" I looked at her puzzled because she knew tonight was movie night just like every other Wednesday since we started school and her ass was coming over whether Tevin liked it or not. I don't know if Cyn noticed it but he was becoming a little possessive when it came to her, but they were just getting back in the swing of things so I wasn't about to say anything.

"Don't look at me like that I was just asking because you know how you get."

"No, bitch, I don't know, you think you're slick but I'm riding with you. Matter fact I'm driving just in case you try to ditch me for my brother." I grabbed the keys from her and unlocked the doors so that we could place our bags in the backseat.

"I wouldn't even do you like that; I love movie night." I ignored her and pulled out of the parking lot, hoping to beat the traffic. Outback was about twenty minutes away and I was craving their coconut shrimp now that Cyn had mentioned it with some steak and mashed potatoes. Yeah that sounded like a plan and I most definitely wasn't cooking tonight, so Ky and Cyn better had jumped on this Outback wave as well.

I bravely hopped out the car without my jacket and the cold air hit me full force and the light weight Nike sweater Cyn and I had in the car did us no justice. People were probably looking at us like we were crazy as we ran from across the parking lot.

"Sis, are you ordering something? I'm not cooking, Cyn." I let her know as we approached the bar to order our food to go. There was no need for us to get a table because I wasn't trying to sit and eat my food here I wanted to eat while we watched whatever shoot 'em up, bang bang movie Cynthia picked today. Sometimes I worried about her and Kymani because when it was their turn to pick movies we always ended watching something violent where someone dies.

"I knew I should have just dropped your ass off first. Now you're not cooking." Cyn could pout all she wanted, but I wasn't stepping a foot in that kitchen tonight and Kymani better hope like hell he ate while he was out because he wasn't answering my text.

We ordered our food and enjoyed an appetizer and a drink while we waited and like always alcohol ran straight through me, so I was dragging Cyn to the bathroom with me. Girl Code 101 'thou shalt never let girlfriend go to the bathroom alone' that was law.

On our way out the bathroom I heard a small voice call out to Cyn, and when I turned around I was speechless.

"Hi, Miss Cynthia." The beautiful little girl spoke as she hugged Cyn and the chick I'm guessing was her mother looked uncomfortable as the two interacted. There was something about the little girl that rang familiar to me, those eyes were the same eyes I looked into every night. When Kymani emerged from the table they were occupying, he looked surprised to see Cyn and I standing there. I mean I was surprised too because I never imagined this being the way I met his daughter. I knew all about Azia from the moment Kymani found out that Talia was pregnant. After a few months, almost a whole year into my bid and coming to the realization that I was indeed sitting up for five years with no chance of early release or parole, I let Kymani know that he was a free man and that I knew there was no way he was going to be able to make it five whole years without the companionship of another woman. I wasn't one of those hopeless romantics who believed that my man could and would stay faithful to me while I was away for five years in a place where if he hugged me for too long the guards were on my back. I knew better and, as much as Kymani tried to deny it at first, he knew better too. I just never thought a baby would come from it. I remember that day like it was yesterday.

"Singleton, let's go you have a visit." I had been inside for about six months and still each time they called me for a visit I grew nervous even though I knew it was only Money.

"Don't be nervous, boo, you look fine." My cellmate, Brittney, told me as I patted my freshly did cornrows that she had blessed me with the night before. Two long big cornrows had become my signature style and Britt always hooked me up. I swear this white chick was so hood she knew all the latest hip hop songs, hairstyles, street lingo, all that and she was from San Francisco. I just knew she had lived in Brooklyn or something in her past life.

"Tell that fine man of yours I said heyy," she joked as I made my way over to Kempner to be cuffed and escorted to

the visiting floor. Ever since this chick Monica spazzed out on her last week, Kempner cuffed us whenever she was transporting us somewhere alone. I didn't blame her because these broads were real life crazy.

"No hard feelings right, Singleton?" Kempner asked as we made our way towards the entrance to the visiting floor and she released me from the cuffs.

"Nah, it's cool, Kemp." See, Kempner was cool as hell and one of the few guards that wasn't on no bullshit in here. Kemp was still talking, but my mind was solely focused on Kymani as I watched him standing, I knew something wasn't right because the smile that he always wore was no longer there. I didn't really get along with my parents, but if something had happened to them I would be hurt. I said a silent prayer as I made my way over to him with an uneasy smile plastered on my face. Just because his mood was off so was mine. Kymani was my other half and whatever affected him affected me.

"Hey, stink," I said once he pulled me into his strong embrace. Since Kemp was on the visiting floor, I knew she wasn't going to trip over our long embrace, so I stood there and basking in the moment. I missed his long hugs and sweet kisses. I knew something was wrong, but I wasn't going to speak on it because when he was ready he'd let it out. I hoped it wasn't Cynthia because she was my only friend outside of Kymani and Tevin, oh shit, Tevin. Nah, my brother was immortal. Bad shit didn't happen to him, bad shit happened to people who fucked with him. My mind slowly drifted to CK and Alana, but as quickly as the thought entered my mind it left because I had just spoken to Alana this morning.

"Wassup, ma, you know I love you right." Was he breaking up with me, I knew I told him it was okay to do him, but six months damn I didn't expect him to dismiss me six months into this five-year bid.

"Don't look at me like that, E. You love me, right?"

"You know I love you, Kymani. Why are you asking me that?" I sat up in the hard chair and braced myself for what was to come next.

"I fucked up, E, I fucked up. I'm sorry." I've seen Kymani cry before but it was very rare so I was taken back by the tears that sat in the corner of his eyes, but refused to fall. I just hoped like hell he didn't fuck up everything we worked so hard to build. There was no way I was going to be able to get through this five years knowing it was all for nothing.

"What happened, Money?" I asked no longer caring about his somber mood because if he fucked that money up I was going to kick his ass.

"Money? Don't even play with me like that, E."

"Just get the shit out already, Ky. What happened?" He reached across the table and grabbed my hands into his and with every word he spoke my heart broke a little inside. As much as he claimed it was a mistake, that didn't change the fact that in nine months he'll be a father to the next bitch's child. I was speechless and the way I was feeling, nothing I said would do us both any good. If it was the other way around and I was sitting there telling him that the next nigga did what only he was supposed to do for me and that's give me a family, he'd probably kill me right then and there and not think twice about it. I know I gave him the green light, I guess I just didn't think it all the way through because with sex came babies.

"I'm sorry, E. I fucked up. I love you and only you and you know that. This shit was a mistake, but I can't let her kill my seed, man, I just can't." I knew that it hurt him to even utter those words to me but it probably hurt me even more.

"I don't know what to say, Ky, I mean I would never ask you to get rid of your child but this shit hurts. What about me? What about us?" I cried as he got up from his seat and pulled me into his arms.

"Kill that noise, bae. It's me and you forever until my casket drops. It'll always be you. I'll always choose you, Erin. Ain't shit changed, but things are going to be a little different and I'm not gon' be no dead-beat ass daddy. I'm going to take care of my responsibilities. I wouldn't be a man if I didn't.

"You wouldn't be my man if you didn't." I had to charge this to the game because there was a bigger picture here. Ky said it was a mistake and I believed him. He never lied to me before and he could have just said fuck Erin and went on about his life and left me to serve out the rest of my sentence without knowing.

"I love you, E."

"I love you too, stink." There was probably nothing that could tear Kymani and I apart and I know whoever the chick was that he knocked up was probably hoping and praying for a happily ever after but once I came home that shit was dead. We sat and talked some more and I didn't bring up the baby situation for the remainder of the visit because it was going to take me some time getting used to. I just hoped like hell she didn't give him his son because when *we used to talk about having kids Ky would always say he wanted his son and that's it, and I wanted to be the one to give it to him.*

"Erin." I heard the little girl say as Kymani introduced us. I was familiar with her voice from all the FaceTime conversations she and Kymani had.

"Hi, sweetie," I spoke as I squatted down to her level. She was the spitting image of Kymani and her long-beaded hair made her even cuter. She could be a poster child if she wanted to and I couldn't front her mother was beautiful too, but Azia favored Kymani more. When I stood up, Kymani grabbed me and pulled me in for a hug, I wasn't trying to make his baby mother uncomfortable, but his ass didn't seem to care as he kissed me. I pulled away because if the shoe was on the other foot nine times out of ten I would have caused a scene but she didn't, not even one word. I'm guessing Kymani was trying to prove a point, but I wasn't about to sit here and play with him and his baby mother.

"I'll see you when you get home, Kymani. It was nice to finally meet you, Miss Azia. Maybe next time we could go and get our hair and nails done together."

"Yayy, okay, Miss Cynthia does my hair. She could do yours too." Cyn and I both laughed, Azia was so innocent and I could tell by the scowl on her mother's face that she was going to be a problem, but as long as she kept that negative energy to herself I was good.

"Erin, this is Talia; Lia this is my wife, Erin." I held my hand out for her to shake and she reluctantly grabbed it back, admiring the princess cut diamond ring that sat proudly on my finger.

"Order 338."

"That's us; later, brother. I'll see you soon, Azia." Cyn hugged Azia and I did the same as she reached out her arms to me.

"You didn't have to blind sis with that big ass rock, E."

"It wasn't intentional. I was just being polite," I said as I grabbed my double order of coconut shrimp and mash. Like always Cyn ate what I ate to make sure I couldn't pick off her plate like I usually did before she caught on to me.

I had texted Tevin earlier letting him know that if he didn't come over for movie night then his ass wasn't eating so instead of stopping by his house we drove straight my house and like the good brother and boyfriend he was, Tevin was there waiting on us. I knew because I saw his car in the driveway next to Kymani's. I didn't expect him to be home that fast I figured he was going to spend some more time with his daughter but when I walked in to an excited Azia I was even more surprised.

"My daddy said that I could spend the night with you and Miss Cynthia if I gave him one hundred kisses, but I don't want to. Can I stay at your house?" She spoke so fast just like Kymani did when he was excited.

"Of course, you can stay." I looked at Ky and he just shrugged his shoulders as him and Tevin sat on the couch watching sports center as always. I walked over to him with my food in hand and Azia hot on my tail. I didn't have a problem with her being here at all, but I did expect him to run it by me first. We just met in the waiting area of Outback now she was in my living room.

"Look at that face, ma, you think I could say no to that." Azia was sitting in between Kymani and I after she made room for herself. There was nothing left for me to say because I had been dying to meet her and now I had the chance I was going to make tonight a night to remember. She wasn't going to go back telling her mom how boring Ms. Erin's house was. Watching Kymani interact with his daughter melted my heart and had me second guessing not wanting kids right now, but I just enrolled in school and a baby wasn't in my plans at all.

"I love you, E." Kymani pulled me close to him while Azia went to wrestle with Tevin. She was such a little busy body and it was cute how she pinned Tevin down and had him begging and pleading to be freed.

"I know." I smirked and as I got comfortable and dug into my food. Outback's coconut shrimp was to die for and once I learned to finesse them myself, they weren't seeing another dime of my money because I was eating there at least three times a month. I felt Kymani staring at me and I knew he was waiting for me to say that I loved him back, but he knew.

***

Instead of one night, Azia ended up staying with Kymani and I for the whole weekend. I didn't know how much fun kids were and Azia was a handful. There was never a dull moment with her because she spoke her mind and was sassy as ever but very respectful and spoiled! I thought I had Kymani wrapped around my finger, but I had nothing on little Miss Azia. She was definitely a daddy's girl and not once since she was here did she cry or act out when Ky had to go out for a few. We did everything from movies to nails to board games. Azia was a joy to be around.

"Hey, stink." I couldn't help but laugh because like every kid Azia picked up on what we said and whenever Kymani walked in the room she would mock me with, 'Hey, stink'.

"A, what I tell you about that? See, E, you done corrupted my princess." Kymani chased after Azia around our bedroom and tickled her.

"Help me! Erin!" Azia's laughter filled our room and I was overwhelmed. Their bond was one I only wished to have with my father, but at five years old I was already reading and writing full paragraphs. I never got the chance to experience this so having Azia around was fulfilling.

After putting them on my Snap, I went over to help Azia. Kymani could always dish it out but he was as ticklish as they came. It was so cute how he always came near tears.

"Aiigh, y'all got it," he yelled as Azia and I continued to tickle him as he squirmed around the bed.

I noticed that Lia hadn't called for Azia since she'd been here, and whenever Azia asked for her, Ky made up some bullshit excuse and offered her something to keep her mind off her mother. I wonder what had happened, but I also felt like it wasn't my place to ask. Lia was Kymani's problem and I had stayed out of it this long, so there was no need for me to intervene now. Today, Azia and I had a hair and nail appointment with Cyn after our horrible attempt to paint each other's nails. Ky had went out and picked Azia up some outfits and the way she loved to dress was super cute. After taking her to Justice one day, I fell in love with the store; they had the cutest outfits.

"I'm ready, stink," Azia said once she walked into my closet as I was looking myself over in the mirror. As much as Ky and I corrected her, Azia still went with 'stink' when referring to either one of us.

"Don't you look cute, Miss Azia." I complimented her graphic tee and ripped jeans.

"My daddy dressed me," she told me as she grabbed my hand and we headed downstairs to where Kymani was waiting on us. He had just gotten a cut, well taper yesterday and his curly tapered fro was everything. When Ky first started letting his hair grow out, I wasn't feeling it but now that he had a little length to it I was all for it.

"Close your mouth, girl."

"Go change your clothes before you make us late," I told him and he smirked like I was playing with his ass.

"Man, I'm not changing shit. Hell, you copped me this sweat suit."

"Yeah for you to wear around me. Not out in the streets; now go change, Ky." I couldn't wear tight fitted jeans and leggings if Kymani wasn't with me, and even if we were together, he didn't like me wearing them and that's how I was when he wore sweatpants. They were the biggest thirst trap and he knew it because one day he sent me a meme from Instagram.

"You dead ass, E?" I wasn't even about to entertain him I grabbed Azia's hand and fished for his keys in his pants pocket and went to get A situated in the car while he went to change his clothes.

Ten minutes had passed and I knew Kymani was taking his time on purpose, and I couldn't help but to laugh when he opened the car door and slammed it shut letting me know he had a whack ass attitude. He changed them pants though. I was just glad he was driving his car today because had he slammed my door like that he would have caught these hands for sure.

"You look nice. Doesn't your daddy look nice, A?"

"You look handsome, Daddy." Azia cutely squealed from her seat and Kymani couldn't hide the big Kool-Aid smile that was plastered on his face. If I had known Ky planned on spending the whole day with Azia and I, maybe I would have let him keep the sweats but then again bitches in the shop were the thirstiest, always trying to get the scoop on that latest hood drama and who was screwing who. Cyn's stylist, Amanda, really irked my nerves and the way she spoke about Tevin and Kymani on first name basis like she knew them always had me wanting to slap some respect into her. Cyn didn't see it, but I didn't trust her ass at all. She was too buddy buddy then wishy washy the next day. A bitch only had one chance to see me and not speak then smile in my face when Ky's around. Nah, that bitch was a dub and I made sure she knew it every time she went out her way to 'Heyy, Erin' me. Kymani would get on me about being rude, but I didn't fuck with sometimey females. Plus, Cyn was all the friend I needed; her multiple personalities had me feeling like I had the luxury of having two to three friends.

My phone went off as I sat there and waited for Cyn to finish Azia's hair. I had already uninstalled my twenty-eight-inches and was more than happy for this blow out I was about to receive. I missed my hair even though my install was everything and next time I was going to try a bob or something exotic, but for now I wanted my hair to breathe a little. I missed how Kymani would play in my hair until I fell asleep.

We should meet up, you can't just erase us out of your life, Erin. We're family, US or Else!

I read the text message over and over and like the other thirty some odd messages that were in the thread. I left them on read. Us or Else was what Junior and I used to say whenever we got in trouble and wouldn't snitch on one another. My father hated how loyal I was to Junior and he despised the fact that I'd rather hang in the projects rather than sit in on debriefings on his current cases. I had nothing against my cousin, Junior, but he was a part of a life that I had walked away from over five years ago, and had up until now done a great job of forgetting they ever existed. Junior was more like me, but he just couldn't walk away from the family. They paid his bills and kept him in the flyest gear, so he sucked up his dreams of becoming a rapper and was now ironically in the same school as me studying to be a psychologist. I wondered what the hell he went through to get out of becoming a part of the Singleton family business in the bureau. Either way, I wanted nothing to do with him or the family. They turned their backs on me because I was different than them and saw that there was more to life

than the fucking FBI! How ironic though, I left my sheltered

life as the daughter of the infamous Special Agent Singleton

to the very life my father and mother despised and spent

their life trying to take down. Five years ago, it was Junior's

dad who tipped me off that they were cracking down on

CK's organization that Ky had just stepped into as the head

nigga in charge. I knew if it was Kymani that walked out of

our apartment in handcuffs. Five years would have been like

a day compared to the sentence they were offering. Like his

son, my uncle Ethan was more cultured and understanding

than my brainwashed ass parents. Ethan was the youngest

of five, and, unlike my father, uncle Ethan knew what it was

like to be in the streets. Before he sold out to the Singleton

name, he was in the streets. CK knew of me before Kymani

because he and my uncle used to be real tight before Ethan

got caught up and my father somehow someway made his

discrepancies disappear as long as he promised to join the

force. I knew I couldn't keep ignoring Junior, so I texted him

letting him know that we'd do lunch one day this week.

When he first started texting me Kymani didn't care either

way if I met up with him because no matter how cool Junior

was, he was still a part of a life that helped steal five years of my life.

Cyn was blowing my hair out when Kymani told me that he was going to sit in the car with Azia because she had fallen asleep in his lap while they waited for me to get my hair done. Cyn couldn't help herself and the honey blonde highlights she added to my hair had me cautious in the beginning, but as she flat ironed my hair the color blended perfectly with my sandy, jet black hair. I swore in the summer my hair was a sandy brown with streaks of blonde but as soon as fall hit, my color faded.

"I have like three more heads, so I'll be here until like eight no later than nine. I know Azia is over there so we could study at my apartment when I get off. I'll just tell Tevin I'm sleeping at home." I looked at Cyn like she had four heads because there was no way she or Tevin was going for that. We could study at my house like we usually did and then she could go home to her crazy ass boyfriend or whatever the hell Tevin was to her. After Kymani told me that he thought Tevin told Cyn to head to Outback on purpose, I wasn't really fucking with him because that was real messy.

"Just call me when you get off, sis. I'll be in the house and Azia will either be in bed or home, Lia was supposed to get her yesterday but that's another story." I kissed Cyn goodbye and stuffed the two hundred dollar bills in her back pocket. I didn't give her a chance to protest like she usually did when I paid her for her services as I quickly exited then shop.

Chapter Nine

Kymani

"Daddy, look what Ms. Erin got me." Azia waved her new book bag in my face. It was a sparkly bag with the letter A on it. Azia had been so excited about starting daycare well school as she called it and she couldn't wait to fill her bag up with all her little cute school supplies. After that week Azia spent at the house with me and E, Lia had been MIA and her mom was calling me off the hook looking for her. I didn't know where Lia was, but I knew she was being spiteful because whenever she called it was Erin this and Erin that. I never took Lia for the jealous type and she knew our situation from jump, we were never in a relationship, but I always respected her as the mother of my child. Lately, Azia had been back and forth from my house to her grandmother's house being that I was out the house majority of the day, handling business, and E had classes during the day. I appreciated Ms. Gomez, but I still didn't like her ass. She was always so judgmental and filling Lia's head up with a bunch of bullshit. I swore Lia got her jealous ways from her mother because if you asked me Ms. Gomez was jealous of her and she was constantly in her ear about some shit she heard about me on the streets.

"Stop spoiling that girl she doesn't even need half that stuff."

"Yes, she does. Plus, it's cute; all girls love sparkly stuff." Azia and E were in the kitchen preparing breakfast before we all started our day. I was sitting at the table with Azia while she showed me all the stuff E had gifted her in her book bag. Today was Azia's first day of daycare and I think I was more nervous than she was.

"You like hanging out with Ms. Erin?"

"Yes, Daddy, I like her. She's so much fun! She lets me do her hair and jump on her bed." Hearing Azia speak so highly of Erin wasn't surprising but I was happy my baby girl liked her. I didn't plan on them meeting the way they did, but I was all for it now. E could have washed her hands with me when I told her about Azia five years ago, but she didn't and now we were here and I've been the happiest now these past few months than I've been in five years.

"Azia, go wash your hands for breakfast." Azia ran towards the bathroom while I helped E set the table for breakfast. This had become a routine for us, well her and Azia, because usually I didn't wake up until it was time for

Erin to leave for class, but today both my girls were off to school.

"You're doing great with Azia, ma, thank you."

"She's a great kid, Ky. Spoiled but a great kid none the less."

"Says the girl that just brought her five new pairs of sneakers and a book bag full of supplies for daycare."

"Shut up."

"Miss Erin, 'shut up' is a bad word remember." I was glad Azia caught her.

"Yes, baby, it is. I'm sorry." Erin kissed her forehead and placed her in her chair. Azia's appetite was crazy. She could body three waffles and eat the whole pack of bacon. Erin had her spoiled with this shrimp and grits every morning or some other fancy shit she was feeding her.

"May I have cheese this time like you?" Azia asked E while she mixed the cheese into her grits. It was like I didn't even exist when Erin was around. I sat back and watched the two of them eat their food and have small conversation about Azia's first day of daycare.

"Good morning, family," Cyn said as she entered the kitchen. I didn't even hear her come in.

"Keep coming in here unannounced and your ass gon' see something you don't wanna see," I told her because ever since E needed Cyn to pick something up from the house she never returned the key and took that as an open invitation to come over whenever she wanted.

"Won't be anything I never seen before. Who's this big girl and what did she do with my Azia?"

"It's me, Auntie, see." Azia waved her bracelet Cyn had given her for her birthday last year in her face.

"What are y'all feeding this girl she's getting taller by the second?" For a five year old, Azia was pretty tall and a lot of times people assumed she was seven or eight. I cleared the table while the girls chatted about whatever girls talked about until it was time to go. Since Cyn was here, I was guessing that E was driving with her and I was taking Azia to school. Lia was supposed to be here for this, but I hadn't heard from her.

"Be a good girl in school and don't forget to say please and thank you. I'll see you later okay, A." E bent down to give Azia a pep talk like she needed any more energy, but Azia was eating it all up.

"Daddy, if Mommy doesn't pick me up, can Miss Erin pick me up?" Erin looked at me in disgust because she felt like I was letting Lia get off too easy, but I couldn't force her to be a mother to her daughter. If she wanted to wait five years to be a dead beat, then so be it. My baby was going to be good regardless. Fuck that bitch, honestly.

"Erin has school too, baby. Maybe next time."

"We'll pick you up and then after we can go get the paint for your new room." Erin let Cyn take Azia to the car and I knew she had some shit to get off her chest.

"So, you think that's it's okay that she hasn't called for her daughter in over a week?

"Like I told you before, E, Lia is a grown ass woman I can't make her be here, especially if her reasoning is you. Nothing or no one should want to keep her from her daughter." I was tired of explaining myself about the same shit when it came to Talia. I knew it had to be some nigga she was fucking with for her to be out here acting like this, but I just couldn't understand why Azia was the one that had to suffer because her mama was trying to make me jealous.

"Ky, you're making excuses for her. There's no way I would let another person raise my kid just because me and my baby father are at odds or whatever the case may be. That's some real weak shit and you know it, and the Kymani I know wouldn't let some shit like that slide, but whatever

I'm going to be late for class. Make sure you remind the teacher of her allergies and asthma. I love you." E pecked my lips and left out without giving me a chance to respond. I was over arguing about Lia anyway I just wanted to get my baby girl to daycare and handle my business for the day.

"I love you, A. Have a good day." I kissed her forehead and waited for her teacher to come to the door.

"I love you too, Daddy." I thought it was going to be hard getting Azia to want to stay in daycare, but I was wrong because as soon as her teacher opened the door A flew inside. She was adjusting well and learning even more. I was on my way to meet up with Chris before I had to head over to the city to meet with Alana about this club she and Erin so desperately wanted me to open. After that Dre situation, I hadn't had any problems from any one on my team and Chris had stepped up big time being that he now ran the trap on his own. Lil' bro was official though and I was spending most of my time schooling him just how CK groomed me. Chris reminded me a lot of myself when I was his age. His hunger and ambition had him out working dudes that have been on my payroll for years. When I walked into the house, it was now semi quiet; only the music from the small speaker in the back could be heard and I shook my head because Chris was a diehard G-Herbo and Lil' Bibby fan, you knew off rip bro was from Chi-Raq how heavy he fucked with them. There were a few people in the house handling their daily duties from cooking and bagging to presentation. My boys, Rock and Bull, were on standby at the door and they were TTG all the way. A nigga couldn't breathe the wrong way in here without them ready to pull their shit back. Nothing moved in here without Chris' approval, he had himself set up in the back room with monitors that oversaw the entire crib and everything in a ten-block radius.

"Wass good, C." I dapped him up and pulled him into a brotherly hug as he stepped away from the table full of money that he was sorting.

"Ain't shit, Money. I ain't even hear you come in, but no funny shit I smelt your pretty ass. When you gon' stop letting wifey have you smelling all sweet and shit." He clowned because E used some fruity ass detergent to wash our clothes, but the shizz smelled hella good.

"Man, when your young ass gets some ass and somebody to take care of you like wifey then you'll be able to smell as fresh as ya boy." I sat down at the table and decided to help him out because I wanted Chris to take that ride with me to meet Alana. Tevin wasn't the best person to bring to a business meeting.

"Damn, C, you pulling in more bank than you were when it was four of y'all. That's a good look, bro, I might have to get you some help over here after all." I was really impressed by the work Chris was putting in at only seventeen he was putting in work like a Vet. I needed Chris to be ready for whatever too, I always threw different shit at him for him to do to make sure that he was ready for whatever that came his way because lil' bro was moving up real soon.

"Nah, I'm good, Money. I work better alone I don't really trust too many niggas other than you and Tee." I respected his word because if my closest friends were able to pull off some snake shit right under my nose, I wouldn't be able to trust easily either.

"Aigh, lock up so we could beat the traffic to the city." He looked at me because there was really no way you could beat traffic to the city unless you took public transportation. On the ride over to the club, I chopped it up with Chris and the more he spoke the more I was able to tell that there was more to Chris than he led on. From the way he spoke, you could tell he had an educational background, and from what he told me, his mother had just gotten laid off from her job

at the clinic and they were forced to move out here and stay
with his aunt over in Brownsville.

"When we go in there I want you to give your honest
opinion. The grand opening is in two days and I need to
make sure everything is straight," I told Chris as we walked
around the block. The spot that E and Alana picked out was
dope as fuck and fully furnished thanks to all the work the
two of them along with Cyn put in over the past few weeks.
It didn't take long for them to get everything together
because the place needed little to no work done since the
previous owner was set to open u last month but came into
some legal issues and couldn't keep up with the payments.
We were lucky as fuck we caught this spot when we did and
the grand opening this Friday was set to be lit. My youngin's
had been promoting it heavy on social media and I had a lot
of heavy hitters on the guest list, so I knew the turn up was
about to be something different.

"How's my daughter?" Alana asked as we stepped inside the
VIP area and Chris looked around admiring the decorum.
"She good you know E. She ain't gon' admit that's
something is bothering her. I know she wants to meet up
with Junior, but is too stubborn to admit it."

"Yeah, she brought it up to me the other night. I think she's waiting on you to tell her it's okay to see him." I had no problem with E meeting up with Junior because that was her family.

Alana walked Chris through the whole set up while I stayed a few steps behind and watched how he handled himself giving his two cents on how he thought a few things should be changed around. My phone was vibrating in my pocket and when I pulled it out I saw that it was E calling as a picture I snapped of her sleeping in the car covered the screen. I slid my finger across the screen to connect the call, but before I was able to say hello Lia's ass was calling.

"Kymani, why is this felon picking up MY daughter? If she wants a kid so bad you better giver her one the same way you did me!" I could hear E and Cyn in the background as Azia cried and Lia continued to show her ass. I knew for a fact there was no way E was going to let Lia get away with disrespecting her like that, but she wasn't going to show out in front of Azia, unlike her unstable ass mama. Man, I wish Lia would have shown me these signs early on. All that private school and boujee shit went right out the window the moment she came face to face with Erin. I hung up on

Lia and called E back to make sure she wasn't about to do anything stupid, but she wasn't answering.

"Put Erin on the phone."

"I don't have time for this shit tell him to call his dirty ass baby mother so I can go the fuck home." I heard E say to Cyn as Azia stood there hanging on to her for dear life. Talia really had to be showing out for Azia to be acting like that.

"That's my daughter, Kymani. You let her turn my daughter against me! I hate you!" Cyn flipped the camera so that I could see how irate Talia was and when my eyes landed on her. The beautiful girl I once knew was no longer, there was something off about her and she looked like she hadn't slept in days.

"Sis, just get E and take my daughter home for me please. I'm on my way."

"I wish I could but twelve just pulled up." I should have known somebody had come to the scene because Lia was now yelling and screaming calling Erin all types of bitches, yet she wasn't doing all that when it was just the three of them out there. I told Cyn not to hang up I wanted to hear everything that was being said. Chris and Alana were now front and center. I guess they heard all the yelling and back and forth. Talia damn sure didn't want any problems with Cyn and E. Their asses weren't wrapped to tight. E just came home off a five-year bid and there was no way she was about to get caught up over my dumb ass baby mama. I had to talk Alana out of not coming with me. Lana was real life crazy and she didn't play when it came to E or CK. I've heard plenty of stories about how she gave it up back in the day and a few of them I've told myself because I was there. Her pistol game was one hundred and there wasn't a female alive that was a match for her hands. She even boxed CK up a few times, but from the outside looking in all you saw was a beautiful well respected and mannered woman and that's exactly how she was raising E to be. When I pulled up to the daycare, I took a deep breath because I didn't fuck with the boys. I had to count down from ten in my head because the look on my daughter's face was a look of fear, and the fact that it was all because of her own mother pissed me off even more. There was no reason for Talia to come out here and show her ass like that. All she had to do was pick up the fucking phone or be around to see her daughter. But of course, today out of all days she decides to show her ass. Both Talia and Erin were on Azia's pick up list so there shouldn't have been a problem with them releasing her to either of them, but because Lia wanted to show her ass and cause a scene they weren't releasing her to either of them. Once I made my way to A's teacher, she told the officer who I was and I was able to take Azia. Him and his partner wanted to question me, but I wasn't beat for that shit right now; I just wanted to take my daughter home.

I had no words for Lia as she stood there looking stupid.

"A, tell mommy you'll see her later," I told her as she held on to my hand tightly and when Azia said nothing I felt bad for Talia because she did this to herself. Her distaste for Erin should have been put on the back burner, especially in the presence of her daughter. Instead of saying bye to Lia, Azia grabbed a hold of Erin's hand. I didn't even feel bad for her ass because Azia hadn't seen or heard from her in weeks and the day she does pop up she decides to show her ass.

"Really, Mani. You're just going to let her walk away with my daughter. I'm not letting you take my fucking daughter, Kymani. I don't think it's safe. She's around a fucking Queen Pin. You left me to go live with a fucking bitch that has been in jail the last five years."

"Watch your fucking mouth when you speak of my wife." The officers were still inside the daycare and Talia was lucky because the shit she was spitting was liable to get her head knocked the fuck off.

"Ky, lets go. She's not even worth it." I could tell that there was more she wanted to say, but opted not to. I knew once we got home I was going to hear her mouth.

When we got home, E took Azia upstairs and got her ready for bed. I couldn't understand why she was mad at me or whatever she called herself doing, but I let her rock out because when we fought, we fought for real; her mouth was too damn slick. She'd say some shit that'll have you rethinking life and ready to ring her little ass neck. Instead of following behind them I made my way to our fitness room and turned the music up so that I could clear my head and release this negative energy

"YFN Lucci's "Letter from Lucci" was on full blast as I lifted weights. Whenever E and I had a disagreement, I found myself in here to avoid us saying some shit that we'd later regret. Arguing the way we did over shit that we couldn't control was one of our biggest flaws. I couldn't understand why she was so against meeting up with her cousin and she didn't like the way I handled Talia. I had no control over Talia's actions, and unfortunately, she had no control over the way her family shitted on her all those years ago, but it was something she needed to face head on rather than run from it. I had a bullet with her pops name on it, but at the end of the day he was E's father and I'd never disrespect her like that because as much as she said she hated him, that was her peoples and she didn't want his blood on her hands. I missed my parents and the life I had before E got locked up. Everything just seemed out of place right now and I had so much built up frustration the 250 pounds I was lifting was nothing to me right now. I thugged out a few more sets and took a break to grab a water from the store like fridge we had installed. I didn't really like the texture of the Evian water that Erin just had to have; I was team Poland Spring all day I didn't care how many studies they ran. When I turned around, I could see Erin standing in the doorway through the wall to wall floor length mirrors we had.

"Where's, A?" I asked her, trying to ease the tension that was between us.

"Sleep for now. She cried herself to sleep. Asking can I be her new mommy. That shit ain't right, Ky. What the fuck is wrong with your baby mother?" I turned the music down since she said Azia was upstairs sleeping. I rubbed my hands over my head because I didn't even have an answer for her.

I honestly didn't know what had gotten into Talia. I mean I knew she was going to be salty over the whole Erin situation I just never thought she'd flip the script like this and drag Azia into her bullshit.

"Don't worry about that, bae, I'm going to handle that I promise. Thank you for not losing your cool in front of baby girl." I walked over to where she stood and inhaled her scent as I stood in front of her. She wondered how I could keep a cool head with Talia showing her ass, well the answer was standing right in front of me. Knowing that I had E in my corner there was no need for me to trip over Lia and her childish ass ways.

"I love you and as long as I have you in my corner, ma, nothing else matters. I don't wanna fight with you over irrelevant ass shit. Azia is lucky to have somebody that cares about her the way you do. I care about you and I want you to know that it's cool if you go meet up with your peoples tomorrow. I'll come with you if you need me to. Cyn and Tevin can watch A until we get back."

"I think that's something I have to do on my own, Kymani, but thank you. I love you more."

"So, you done being mad at me or whatever? I almost fucked you up, I heard all the slick shit you were saying to Cyn. And I love you more, not more than you love me, but more than all the bullshit and irrelevant shit that has been thrown our way. I love you more than I love myself. Now let me feed my babies then we could work on making A a little brother." I pulled her close to me and kissed her forehead, sweat dripping down my head and all.

"Eww, Kymani, why would you do that," she whined as she tried to pull away from me only for me to hold her in place." Future and Usher's "Rivals" played in the background while I held Erin in my arms. I sang along to the song as she rested her head against my chest.

I just love the times when I'm beside you

Holding me down 'cause you my rider

I look in your eyes and I get higher

'Cause nothing in this world I hold tighter

Without you I feel uneven

Make every day, our love season

Baby girl, you know you're my rider

That should be enough reason

Call you baby, that's only your title

'Cause I don't need no more rivals

I put that on the Bible

T'yanna Sha-Nay

You're the only thing that I want

All I wanted to do was take all her pain away and rid her life of all the bullshit that was thrown our way. From day one, I vowed to be there for her and introduce her to nothing but the finer and better things in life, I never wanted my bullshit to cause her harm or discomfort.

Chapter Ten

Kymani

It just seemed like when I thought shit couldn't get any worse it did. First Talia and her bullshit, now three of my traps were hit at the same damn time. I couldn't win for losing these days, and I low-key felt like niggas were testing my gangster. These had to be some new niggas or some shit because everybody in the five boroughs knew how I gave it up.

"Something about this shit don't feel right, bro," Drayco said and I couldn't agree with him more, but I didn't know what the fuck was going on. All I knew was that three of my houses were hit and I was missing out on money and product. The first time in over five years my spots were hit other than that Dre situation. I was confused as to who was gunning for me because I broke bread with everybody. There wasn't a soul on my team that went without and whoever wanted to get put on and was real right, I broke bread with them too as long as they stayed in their lane.

"We need to call a meeting, bro. Gather all these niggas up and see what's what." Tevin wasn't as angered as I was and I guess he was saving his energy for the niggas that decided to cross us. I took a pull from the blunt that sat between my lips and tried my best to keep my cool. The money they got me for was nothing compared to what I had in my stash house, but it was the principle that a motherfucker even had the balls to run up on me and mines.

First Dre and his buddies got me for 25k that I didn't even get a chance to get back, and now I was losing even more money because I had to close up shop. With everything going on, I needed to make sure that E and Cyn were straight and after the way Tevin showed his ass last night. I knew sis wasn't fucking with him right now, so it was my responsibility to make sure they were good. Between Lia and Tevin, I don't know who showed their asses more last night; they both deserved donkey of the day if you asked me. Drayco rode with me over to the house to check on the girls while Tevin met everyone over at the warehouse.

Pulling up to the warehouse where we usually held our meetings, I watched everyone's demeanor and how they eyed Drayco because he was a fresh face. All my niggas were on ninety and I couldn't see one of them having anything to do with the shit that transpired from last night to this morning. As I made my way through the warehouse, I greeted everyone in passing. They showed respect and saluted me as I made my way through. When I spotted Tevin, he was chopping it up with one of his workers at the head of the table and I saw the look he gave Dray as we approached him and I wasn't sure how much longer he was going to let Tee throwing shade his way slide, but I hoped he was the bigger person and let that shit ride at least until I figured this shit out. I stood and waited for Tevin to remove himself from my seat then sat down before saying anything like I usually did when we held a meeting.

"Aiigh, everybody, this is my brother, Drayco, and he's going to be sticking around for a while until we get this shit figured out. Everything that has happened in the past forty-eight hours won't happen again. There will be a rotation amongst the houses and everybody will be held accountable for their shifts. Dray, Tee, and Chris are the only people that will handle deliveries and drop offs. We're in this shit to stack money, not let that shit slip away right before our eyes. Y'all gotta tighten up and keep y'all ears to the streets. Anybody get word on who hit my shit, I want to know immediately!" I knew Tee wasn't happy about Drayco sticking around, but he was going to have to boss the fuck up and the look on his face right now had me questioning my man for the first time in over ten years.

"I don't need no fucking babysitter, Money. That's your man's not mine and there ain't shit he could possibly do for me, so all that partnership shit you spitting you might as well save that shit, fam," he said in a matter of fact tone. Little did he know this wasn't up for debate. He should be lucky Drayco offered his help in the first place because obviously, he wasn't doing such a good job at running his shit on his lonely.

When I gave Tee full control of the traps while I took a step back and dealt directly with CK and the money, it was like shit was going bad left and right and I was done with motherfuckers playing with my bread. This meeting was over as far as I knew, so I dismissed everyone and Chris and Drayco stayed behind so that we could go over a few things that needed to be adjusted moving forward. Instead of Tevin being about his business, his cry baby ass stormed out with an attitude. I wasn't in the business of pacifying him anymore. It was time for him to grow the fuck up and be my right-hand man. We needed to put all of our energy into the motherfuckers that were taking money out of my lady's pockets.

After rearranging a few things and giving Chris more responsibility than he was used to since Tevin was in his feelings, I was on my way home to lay up with my lady. All day E was all I thought about because I knew if she was on board one hundred percent, half of this shit wouldn't have been happening. When I walked in the house, E was laid out on the couch watching *Paid in Full*. I was surprised she wasn't in the theater room.

"What you doing up here, ma?" She sat up, allowing me room to sit down and I pulled her into me as she rested her head on my chest, probably counting how many times my heart beats in a minute or some weird shit like that. I knew because that's what I would do. I studied everything about her, and although not much has changed, I was learning everything about E all over again. What made her smile, cry, happy, everything.

"I knew I smelt something burning." I clowned as I pulled her up so that she was now sitting on my lap and facing me.

"Why must you play all day? I should have just let your ass starve."

"I was just kidding, ma. You know you're Top Chef in the Martin household."

"Why are you staring at me like that?" E wasn't uncomfortable but I could tell my intense gaze was affecting her.

"I love you, E. More than anything in this world. If anything was to ever happen to me just know everything I did was for us and the life we used to dream about living. I'd do all this shit over again for you, just to make you happy, ma. I can't repay you for everything you've done to make sure that we were straight and everything you're still doing to make sure that my shorty is good too."

"I love you more, stink. Why are you saying all this? You're making me nervous."

"I need a reason to tell you how much I love you now? What you cooking? I haven't eaten since this morning." I smiled thinking about the fun we had in the shower this morning. E's sexual appetite was nothing to play with. I swore she was trying to make up for lost time and I was all for it because I knew my son was going to come from all this as much as she wanted to deny it.

"BBQ chicken, baked macaroni and cheese, and steamed vegetables." E ignored my comment and led the way to the kitchen where she began making my plate.

"You're not eating?"

"I had a late lunch with Azia after I picked her up today. I'll probably eat some later." E sat my plate down in front of me and sat down on my lap. Her ass was so spoiled, I couldn't even eat in peace.

"Ma, how you expect me to eat with you on my lap?"

"Like this." She forked a piece of the baked macaroni and fed it to me. We sat there until my plate was clean and E fed me every bite while we talked about everything I still had to do for the grand opening. Cyn and Erin had been a big help with making tomorrow a night to remember.

"How much this shit going for, bra?" Chris asked the young boy with his Chicago accent on full display. When he called me a few hours ago, about some young boy reaching out about some work they wanted to get off, I was tight I had to leave E, but there was more pressing matters in the streets that we needed to tend to. I didn't want to risk one of them recognizing me, so I stood off to the side with my fitted cap pulled down low so that my eyes were barely showing and listened to this amateur boast about getting the come up of their lives.

"I have about fifteen right here 'cause we ain't know what y'all niggas were trying to cop, but trust there's more where this came from. For you, fifteen because I respect the next man trying to come up." Not only did this little nigga rob me of my product, but he was letting my shit go for almost forty percent less than what it's worth. We were going to play along with them though because I wanted all my work back.

"Say that, bra, so let me clean house and get everything you got," Chris said and I watched as their eyes widened and greed took over rather than common sense. There was no way I was selling all my shit for almost half the price to some niggas I didn't even know.

"Let me make a call to my brother and I'll have him get everything ready for y'all," the young boy said as I tossed a duffle bag full of money on the table. We were up in the Bronx and I wondered how these little niggas even got wind of my operation because I didn't even do business in the Bronx like that. Only Tee did because that's where he was originally from. These young boys couldn't have been older the sixteen or seventeen, but he was portraying himself to be as legit as they came. I knew better though, thankfully because there was no way any real hustla was letting his shit go for less than seventeen.

"My brother is going to meet up with us, come on." The young boy spoke up and started re-bagging my work in his duffle bag.

"Really appreciate this, bra, I need to get this shit on the streets ASAP. If your brother comes through I might have a little incentive for you." Again, he got overjoyed and started showing off all thirty-two of his big ass teeth. If they were smart instead of trying to get the work off their hands, they would have sold the shit themselves to get a greater profit but I guess it was only about the money for him and whoever the fuck his brother was.

Little man ain't even have a ride, so he had to ride with us. Another mistake. I just shook my head and made sure my pistol was where it was supposed to be and drove a few blocks down to this abandoned like house. For a minute, I thought he was setting us up because this whole block looked suspect but when he exited our car and walked over to an old beat up Honda like the one I used to drive back in the day and grabbed two more duffle bags, I was glad. Playtime was over though because now I had all my product back.

"Good looking, lil' bro," I said as I pulled my hat to the back so that he could see my face clearly, and I saw it was like he was seeing a ghost.

"Aye, Money, man, I'mmm I-I'm sor-rrryy." I was surprised he knew who the fuck I was, but even more so disappointed because his ass knew who I was and still jacked me for my shit.

"Save that sorry shit for someone who cares." I raised my pistol with the silencer attached, not like I needed it on this dead ass block, but still I didn't need to bring unnecessary attention to the situation. He was rambling a whole bunch of shit and I just figured he wanted to get some shit that I didn't want to hear.

PEW! PEW!

PEW! PEW!

Two to the head and he was out for the count. I'm guessing Chris was tired of hearing his rambling as well because he let off two shots at the exact same time as me if not a little earlier. I looked at him and shook my head with pride though because my young boy was just as ruthless as I was.

"Lil' bra, was probably repenting for his sins. Let's get out of here before a crackhead come out of one of these houses or some shit." Chris grabbed one duffle bag and I grabbed the other and we tossed them in the backseat of my Tahoe before pulling off and heading back to Queens. I called Dray and told him to meet us at the spot and got Tee's voicemail for like the tenth time today. I wasn't about to chase his ass like I had to do since we were kids when he didn't get his way, but nah, not tonight there was too much shit going on for me to have to worry about Tevin and his bipolar ass right now.

***

Chapter Eleven

Tevin

Everything was finally falling into place and was finally seeing progress in my plan to take over Money's whole operation. He thought by bringing Drayco out here that was going to slow up my show, but that only made it easier for me to move because with Dray here Money would be paying less attention to me and what I was doing.

"Hey, Tevin." I heard a familiar voice say behind me, as me and Ahmad were chilling in front of my old building waiting for his little brother to hit us up once he got the money from these niggas he knew that were trying to buy the work we just got off the trap houses. I could have easily just took the shit, but I wasn't a dummy and I needed it to look like someone was coming for our spots in the streets.

"Wassup, Amanda." I was surprised she even spoke to me after the way I dismissed her ass in the elevator at the hospital. The PINK leggings she wore had her phat ass on full display for everyone to see. I was in a good mood, so I didn't mind giving her a little conversation.

"Yo, I'm about to go drop this shit off. I'm gonna hit you when I'm done," Ahmad said as he hopped in his ride and pulled off before I got a chance to say anything.

"You seem to have some time on your hands, why don't you come upstairs and we could chill or whatever." I looked down at her and smiled because I knew exactly what her definition of chill was. I had a few drinks earlier after I left the warehouse and that dirty sprite shit that Ahmad had passed me a few minutes ago had me on another level. Yeah, I loved Cyn, but lately she had been so busy with school and up Erin's ass that it was fuck me and what I needed. After this shit was all over, Cyn was going to be a distant memory anyway because I knew for a fact she was going to choose them over me.

Amanda was in the middle of handling my Jr. when my phone rang and seeing that it was Ahmad I answered on the first ring.

"They shot him! They killed my fucking little brother," Ahmad yelled into the phone and I pulled my dick from down Amanda's throat and fixed my clothes.

Fuck, just when I thought shit was looking up some bullshit happens. When I pulled up on Ahmad, he was standing over his brother's lifeless body yelling and screaming at the air. I shook my head at the sight before me because this little nigga just fucked up my whole plan. I looked in the trunk praying that whoever caught him slipping didn't get the work that was in the trunk of the car.

"It was Money, man. I seen the shit with my own two eyes. He pulled up with Twan, split his shit, took the work, and dipped. I watched him kill my little brother man what the fuck!" Ahmad continued to yell while I stood there unbothered. My whole plan was fucking tarnished because of his dumb ass brother.

"I thought you checked the dudes he was making the drop with before the shit went down!" I yelled not understanding how this shit went wrong.

"I did. It was some little nigga from Chicago. He had just moved down here with his mans and they were looking for a come up."

"They played your dumb ass. That was Chris, Money's new protégé. I can't believe your ass was so dumb, Mad."

"How the fuck was I supposed to know that? If your ass wasn't so afraid of the nigga we wouldn't be in this shit in the first place," he spat, getting in my face.

"Nigga." I pulled my pistol from my waist and raised it to his head.

"I've never been afraid of nan nigga, fuck you and your dead ass brother," I yelled as I cocked my gun ready to split his shit so that he could join his dumb ass brother. Before I could pull the trigger, Ahmad drew back and hit me with some shit. I stumbled back a bit and reached over and hit Ahmad upside his head with my nine. I wasn't about to fight with this dumb ass nigga I needed to see how much this nigga Money knew about the whole situation.

Letting off three shots to his chest and one to his head, I left him stinking right next to his brother.

"FUCK!" I yelled as I banged my hands against the steering wheel. Everything was just great, now everything was all fucked up, and it was my fault for trusting niggas to do some shit I needed done my way.

"You's a trifling ass nigga, yo." I heard someone say from the backseat of my car. When I looked through the rearview mirror, I saw the nigga Drayco sitting back there hoodied up with two nines sitting on his lap.

"Nigga, fuck you! You don't know shit about me!" I yelled discretely trying to conceal the weapon I still had in my hand.

"After everything Money did for you. This how you repay him, Tee?" Everything was always about Money; everybody always cared about fucking Money.

"If you was real about your shit, you wouldn't even be having this conversation with me I'd be dead."

"Trust if I wanted to kill you, bro, you'd be dead a long time ago. You don't even deserve to be breathing right now, but my man deserves to know why a nigga he trusted with his life snaked him for a few bricks and some Burger King cash." How the fuck this white motherfucker got in my shit without me seeing him was beyond me.

"Aye, man, just get this shit over with," I spat, gripping my gun trying to find the right time to split this niggas head in two. Fuck it.

BOC! BOC!

I sent two shots flying in the backseat and prayed that I hit his ass as I jumped out the car and made a run for it. Drayco had crazy aim because without even leaving the car the nigga hit me in my thigh twice as I ran down the alley way. I could hear him coughing up what I hoped was blood.

"Aye, Amanda, I need you to come meet me," I said into the phone trying not to focus on the pain that was taking over my body.

Faith in my Hustla

Faith in my Hustla

Faith in my Hustla

Faith in my Hustla

Chapter Twelve

Cyn

When I got the call that Tevin had been shot, I was traumatized and I immediately rushed over to the hospital to be with him. I had been at the shop for a few hours and I was only on my first client. Today felt like it was never going to end because I had about four more heads to do and that wasn't counting the walk-ins. I loved what I did but being on my feet for hours on end wasn't what I called a good day's work. I always loved doing kids' hair because of the joy it brought when they looked in the mirror and thanked me over and over for making their hair so pretty.

"Bitch, you're supposed to be my friend! You sat there and held my hand while I sat in the emergency room after this nigga beat my ass and listened to me cry about how he was dogging me in the streets. When you started working for the bitch he left me for, I didn't trip. But for you to fuck the same nigga you acted as if you couldn't stand is real fucked up!" I didn't understand what was going on, nor did I understand why either of them were here. I watched as Tevin's old flame, Shaniece, charged at Amanda while a few of my stylists stood in between them.

Faith in my Hustla

"Oh, look it's the lady of the hour. I bet you didn't know your little stylist over here was fucking OUR man either," Shaniece yelled belligerently then somehow broke free from the hold the security guard had on her and delivered a combination of blows to Amanda's face. The look she wore on her face gave me all the answers I needed. What I didn't understand was why Shaniece was so hell bent on who Tevin was fucking when she just had a baby by that old ass white man from College Point.

"Bitch, you're just mad that baby wasn't his and he dismissed you at the hospital. I don't give a fuck about what you're talking about." Amanda and Shaniece were now in a full-blown fight in the waiting room, while I stood there looking like the dumbest bitch alive as two females fought in the waiting room of the hospital over MY nigga.

I didn't even waste my time addressing either of these corny bitches and went inside the room the nurse said Tevin was in.

I was sick of him shitting on me left and right. The whole Niecy thing wasn't a surprise to me because I knew all about her and the baby he told me that much, but fucking

205

Amanda, a bitch that I spoke to everyday and signed her checks that was just straight up disrespectful.

When I pulled up, I went straight for the garage and grabbed the steel bat from my truck and started fucking his shit up. Every car from his Benz to his Porsche, I was busting the windows out his shit like Jazzmine Sullivan. I had realized a long time ago that Tevin didn't really love me. He loved the thought of me only loving him and no one else. He was so possessive and insecure that whenever we went out, he accused me of checking other dudes out or looking for attention when that was never the case, but if I caught him staring at a chick for a little longer than respectful he chalked it up to him being a nigga.

I took my time on his Benz because this was his favorite car and I knew he'd be real hurt when he walked in and saw his most prized possession all fucked up. It was time for me to live for Cyn and fuck what Tevin had to say or how he felt because he didn't give a fuck about me and mines. Once I was satisfied with my handy work, I went inside and packed my bags, after taking all his clothes and filling up the tub with bleach and dumping them inside with his sneakers, too. I took his key off the ring of my keys and tossed it on the dresser near a picture of us that, I had just smashed off the wall.

I knew I couldn't go home because that would be the first-place Tevin would come looking for me, so I checked myself into a hotel and called Erin once I made it to my room. Ky and Tevin were like brothers and I knew if he called asking for me, Kymani's loyalty was to his brother so I wasn't risking staying at their house either.

"Cyn, what the hell happened, your hands are bleeding," E yelled worriedly as she wrapped a rag around my bleeding hands. The small cuts on my hands were nothing compared to the hurting Tevin had put on my heart, and I hadn't even realized them until E mentioned it. I told myself I wasn't going to cry, but all of that went out the window when I finally got a chance to sit down and take in everything that had transpired.

"I told you I never trusted that bitch, just wait until I catch her ass," E boasted once I told her what happened at the hospital less than two hours ago.

"Fuck her, sis, I'm not worried about either of them broads on God. I'm done with your brother, I can't keep putting myself through this shit."

"What I can't believe is how you fucked his shit up like that." I had taken pictures of my work and sent them to her as I drove over to the hotel.

"I should have saved all my energy for his ass is what I should have done. I know you probably don't believe me, E, but I'm serious he fucked Amanda. Out of all the bitches he could have messed around with, he chose somebody I saw every day, spoke to, and conversed with. She wasn't my friend and I know her and Niecy had history, but I didn't expect this shit." I didn't tell E about Tevin being in the hospital because I didn't give a fuck about him or his situation anymore. I knew Kymani got that call the same way I did and she could find out from him. Right now, I just wanted to enjoy my best friend and forget all about the bullshit that came with Tevin Marquis Daniels.

That's what I got for putting my trust in people so easily. The tears fell from my face freely ass E held me in her arms and I cried my little heart out. I knew it wasn't going to be easy getting over Tevin, but I was making the first step by removing myself from the situation. I couldn't keep playing the dummy and allowing him to walk all over me and forgive him just because I loved him. I loved myself more though and for the first time in years I was okay with Tevin not being a part of my future. Tevin really had me thinking everything was all good and that we were building something but fucking Amanda, whether it was recently or not, was a deal breaker for me because he allowed that bitch to smile in my face like everything was all good.

The Miseducation of Lauryn Hill played in the background as I laid my head in E's lap and she played in my hair doing her best to calm me down.

***

I had over a hundred missed calls from Tevin and I was guessing he made it home and saw that all his shit was fucked up. After blocking his number, I stretched and made my way to the bathroom to get ready for tonight. E had left a few hours ago, when Ky called and I was left here all alone. I pushed all the bullshit out of my head and ran my bath as I lit a few candles around the bathroom and turned out the light to set the mood. Beyoncé's *Lemonade* played through the speakers while I sank deeper in the hot water with my glass of wine. I was in a good space right now and that nap did me justice, my headache was no longer a problem. "Sorry" was my favorite song on the album and I sang along to the words while I sipped on my wine.

He trying to roll me up (I ain't sorry)

T'yanna Sha-Nay

I ain't picking up (I ain't sorry)

Headed to the club (I ain't sorry)

I ain't thinking 'bout you (I ain't sorry)

Me and my ladies sip my d'usse cups

I don't give a fuck chucking my deuces up

Suck on my balls pause

I had enough

I ain't thinking 'bout you

After listening to the song three times, I allowed the water to drain and turned the shower on so that I could wash my body. Keish had installed a long thirty-eight-inch weave in my head a few days ago, and I was loving the way the fiery red hair hung from my head. I never did color before and I let E talk me into going red and I think it was the best decision I had ever made with my hair. The black, strapless dress I wore had me feeling myself even more and I knew once Tevin saw me he was going to blow a gasket, because when I brought this dress home he told me I wasn't ever stepping out the house in it. Had we been together right now, I would have never put it on, but it was fuck Tevin from here on out and I was stepping out tonight. I placed my jewelry on and the way the diamond necklace glistened on my neck had me feeling myself even more.

I sent E a text letting her know that I was ready and I would meet her in the city. I knew there was a possibility that Tevin was going to show up and that baby ass bullet wound wasn't going to stop him from trying to get at me for ignoring his calls, but he fucked up and I wasn't sorry.

E's home girl, Brittney, was up here with her fine ass brother, Drayco, and sis was cool as hell. It was only the two of us up in VIP with a bunch of niggas as we waited for the lady and man of the hour to show up. Brittney and I were vibing and dancing to the music and throwing back shots of Patron when we heard the DJ yell over the speakers that Ky and Erin were in the building.

"Hey, brother, congratulations." I hugged Ky and we both watched as Brittney and E embraced loudly. Brittney was Erin's surprise from Kymani, even with tonight being about him and the grand opening Ky still found a way to make this about E and I oved that about him. He was always looking out for her while Tevin was always looking out for self. I was guessing he hadn't heard about the shooting because the only way I found out was because one of my clients worked at the hospital and was there when Amanda brought Tevin in. I know he needed to know about his boy, but Tevin was fine I made sure of it before I left and went to go fuck up his shit.

The grand opening was a success just like I knew it would be but when I spotted Lia in the crowd of people that were on the dance floor I knew some shit was sure to pop off because the bitch had time to come out and party but not come see her daughter. I guess E caught my eyes and she was heading in the direction where Lia was talking to a few other chicks with me and Brittney right behind her. Kymani was upstairs with Chris and his team and they were all up there enjoying themselves. Only person missing was Drayco, and neither Brittney nor Kymani knew where he was. When I first met Drayco, a few days ago when he came to town, I was infatuated with his persona, but I pushed my lustful thought of him out my mind because I was over messing with Kymani's friends.

"What the fuck are you doing here?" Lia asked surprised like she didn't know whose establishment she was in.

"Are you dead ass? You could come to the grand opening of Kymani's club, but you can't call and check up on your daughter?" E spoke in a matter of fact tone.

"This is not Kymani's event. It's Money's." Now if I didn't already think this bitch wasn't dumb, I knew for sure she was now.

"Who is this bitch?" Brittney asked.

"Azia's dead beat ass mama. Who doesn't even know who her child's father is."

"Try doing a background check next time, ma, before you lay on your back for a nigga." I'm guessing Ky got wind of what was going on because I saw him approaching us with a scowl on his face.

"Wass good, Money?" Brittney said to Ky as he grabbed E by the waist.

"What's going on? Lia, what the fuck you doing here?"

"So, you're Money? The man I've been hearing all this big talk about. I'm just wondering when you were going to tell me, the MOTHER of your child, about your other life."

"Bitch, he doesn't have to explain himself to you. Matter fact, get the fuck out of here with all that hand talking and shit before you get fucked up."

"Fucked up, by who? The jailbird that's trying to raise my daughter. Imagine that."

WHAM WHAM WHAM

E was raining blows on Lia and there was nothing any of us could do about it because when E turned up it was a wrap. I hated it had to be right now but this was long overdue. E allowed Lia too many chances to come out her face towards her. I was hoping one of her friends wanted to jump bad, but they stood off and watched their home girl get her ass handed to her. Ky did too for a minute before grabbing E off Lia and picking her up off her feet.

"Aye, bra, we gotta dip. Dray in the hospital he got shot up in the Bronx or some shit like that," Chris said as he ran up on us.

"Fuck!" Kymani screamed as he put E on her feet and grabbed her hand as we all rushed out of the club. So much for me turning up tonight. Today couldn't get any worse. First Tevin, then Lia, and now Drayco. Brittney was ready to paint the whole city of New York red for her brother. She was on some Money Mitch shit when they kidnapped his little brother, Sunny.

Chapter Thirteen

Erin

It felt weird waking up without Azia jumping on the bed trying her hardest to wake me and Ky up. Alana and CK were keeping her until Sunday, and although I missed her, I was glad because after the night we had last night I just wanted to lay in bed all day and get my butt rubbed, but Kymani wasn't taking Drayco being in a coma to lightly, so he was hitting the streets and talking about getting Dray moved to a better hospital. I knew it had a lot to do with his traps getting hit and the shooting that left Drayco in the hospital in a coma and Tevin wounded. I didn't understand why Cyn didn't find the need to tell us that Tevin was in the hospital, but on the other hand, she was in her feelings so I kind of did understand where she was coming from.

Go treat yourself, ma. Not that you need any more clothes but fuck it. I don't want you sitting in the house all day by yourself. I'm going to be out for a min maybe a day or two so keep Britt occupied and Cyn too.

Money!

It was little stuff like this that made it so easy for me to fall deeper in love with Kymani. With everything going on in his life right now, he still made time for me and made me feel like the luckiest girl in the world. I read the note that he left on the bed in the space where he once occupied before he left me here alone and couldn't stop the smile that spread across my face. I laid on Kymani's side of the bed and sniffed his pillow before getting up to start my day. Retail therapy was just what Cyn and I needed I knew after the night we had. I sent her a text telling her to get ready and I would pick her up on my way.

I loved that Kymani always took the time to make me feel special. Putting the note down next to the four stacks of hundreds, I pulled myself out of bed and gathered my things for my shower.

Cyn: Rain check, Laila Ali, I have a hangover.

I never expected to put hands on Talia last night, but her mouth was just too reckless and I just knew the bitch had hands to back herself up, but boy was I wrong. Kymani gave me a piece of his mind once we got home after leaving the hospital for showing my ass the way I did. I didn't feel bad for putting her in her place.   When I pulled up to Roosevelt Fields Mall, I shook my head at all the people that were out today. I swore this mall stayed packed. Once I found parking, I had to take a minute to familiarize myself with the mall before I ended up getting lost. I was leaving out of the Louis Vuitton store and the sight before me had me speechless. A man I once loved and adored now looked at me with hate filled eyes, it was crazy because I smelled him before I even saw him, the Gucci Guilty cologne was all too familiar to me.

"Erin, baby, is that you? Oh, my God!" Elaina yelled as she rushed over to me and pulled me into a hug that was supposed to make me feel whole again. A hug that was supposed to exemplify the love of a mother and daughter, yet I felt as if a stranger was holding me in their arms for dear life. My words were caught in my throat and truthfully, I didn't know what to say or if I should even say anything. I had texted Junior earlier, letting him know I was going to be at the mall, and I couldn't help but to feel like this was a set-up, only thing was that Junior was nowhere to be found.

"Hey, Elaina," I dryly spat stepping back and putting space between us as I stared her and my father dead in their face.

"Erin, that's no way to address your mother, have some respect," Mister firmly stated as he finally acknowledged me. I hadn't heard my father's voice in over seven years and I didn't miss it one bit. Everything about him turned me off and growing up, I was daddy's little girl so it was kind of weird standing here in front of him and not sharing the love I once had for him. There was so much tension in the store I think even the shoppers noticed as they stopped and stared a little as the three of us stood there in an intense stare down with no words spoken.

"Mother? I hadn't had a mother since I was a freshman in high school. If you two don't mind I have places to be." I wanted nothing more than to get out of here and back in my comfort zone in a life where Mister and Elaina Singleton didn't exist.

"Places like where? Back with that low life boyfriend of yours, huh. I see you still haven't learned your lesson."

"Oh, you mean the low life that took me in and fed and clothed me? The one who was there for me more that my so-called parents ever were? I don't even know why y'all stopped to talk to me. I thought I was dead to you?" I wanted to remind my father of the last thing he said to me seven years ago.

Erin, you walk out that door and you're dead to me. You hear me, Erin; dead to me!

Faith in my Hustla

"It's time for you to come home, Erin. I've let you go for long enough and look where that has gotten you. Do you know how embarrassing it is to walk into work every day knowing most of the men in my office helped put you away?"

"Erin, baby, just come home we could work this out," Elaina sobbed and I couldn't front though, seeing my mother for the first time in years did something to me.

I loved this lady like no other and still she let my father run her life and mine. Why couldn't she protect me? Why didn't she fight for me? Why couldn't they understand that just because I was different than them, and that I was still their child and deserved to be loved? There were so many questions that I had that went unanswered because Elaina Singleton didn't speak unless she was given permission to. I didn't understand the hold my father had on her and the rest of the family, but I wasn't up for his shit today.

"You had your whole life planned for you, yet you chose to run away and into the arms of a low life dope boy or whatever the fuck they call themselves these days and ended up doing five whole years in the very place I take pride in sending low lives."

There were a few nights I laid in my cell and cried for my father, not the man that stood before me today, but the man that used to hold me in his arms until I fell asleep. The man that attended every father daughter dance from Kindergarten to seventh grade. As much as I despised him, I needed my father growing up. I needed my family well, I thought I needed them, because my life with Kymani was better than any life he had planned for me. No one knew of the hell I went through under the roof of Mister Singleton, but Junior and still he thought it was a good idea to bring them here. I knew coming here was a mistake.

"And I'd do it all over again if it pissed you off that much. As much as you despise Kymani, he's always been there for me and never once turned his back on me. He was the mother and father I needed and I love him for reasons you won't understand because you still think the world revolves around you, Dad! But what about me? Huh, what about your daughter, not once did you ever ask what I wanted to do or how I felt it was always Erin do this or Erin will be that! I hated you and how you treated me, but I loved you because you were my father and hating you wasn't even worth the trouble anymore because I couldn't change you or make mom woman enough to stand up for her daughter let alone her damn self."

"Erin, you don't have to be so mean." Elaina spoke up and I couldn't hold back the laughter that erupted because she truly seemed hurt.

"I don't have time for this shit. You don't have to be so damn blind! Fuck you and that piece of shit you worship so much. I'm good, I don't need or want for anything from either of you trust that and Junior lose my number," I spat as I spotted him slow creeping around the corner.

I just knew it wasn't a coincidence that they happened to be at the mall the same time I was supposed to meet up with him. I took one last look at my parents and shook my head before walking away. I no longer held hatred in my heart for either of them, yet I felt bad for them. I was over feeling sorry for myself because my family wasn't shit but a bunch of quota meeting, fake ass individuals. The bureau was all that they cared about and being the daughter of Mister Singleton, I was supposed to abide by every rule and I knew that five years hurt him more than it hurt me because of all the backlash he got in the press and from his colleagues.

"You're on your own now, you ungrateful little bitch," he shouted.

Once I made it to my car I didn't even have the energy to cry or feel anything from the conversation that just transpired between me and my so-called parents. The only mother I knew was Alana Davis and she was all I needed. I heard someone tapping on my passenger side window and when I looked over it was Junior.

"I'm sorry about all that, E. I ain't think he was going to come here on that bullshit. I'm sorry I wasn't there for you while you were locked up, but I couldn't get to close if I wanted to keep my job. Just know I always made sure that you were good. In this box is something I should have let you hear five years ago, but the timing wasn't right. After you listen to it, destroy it." Junior dropped the box on the passenger seat and walked away.

Curiosity got the best of me and I tore the box open to see what was inside and when a tape recorder fell out I hit play. Hoping that there wasn't any bullshit about Kymani on here, I had enough heartbreak for one day.

"Damn, girl, you keep pleasing a nigga like that I might have to tie your ass up and keep you for myself."

"Good looking, Ken, but you got to get up out of here the nigga, Money, on his way over here and he be tripping off having bitches in our shit."

"Fuck, Money, you're the head nigga in charge/ I don't know why you still keeping his ass around anyway. Stick to the plan, Tee." The woman spoke up and for the life of me I couldn't put a face behind the voice and that angered me.

"I just need a little more time, him and that bitch he's been parading around here are the reasons why your ass is laced in Gucci and Prada, but trust I have some shit in the works for his ass."

"Like what, getting him locked up? That shit didn't work because that bitch you're talking about turned herself in last night," the female voice snapped.

"The fuck, it was supposed to be him, not her! Damn those pigs said they weren't going to move until I gave the okay!" I could hear the fear in Tevin's voice and the first time in the eight years that I've known Tevin, I had hatred in my heart for him. I shook my head as tears fell from my eyes uncontrollably, I couldn't stand to listen anymore, so I turned the tape off and tossed it in my purse.

"Cyn, I need you to meet me at the house ASAP," I spoke into the phone once I pulled out of the parking lot and our FaceTime was connected.

I wanted so badly to stop for Shake Shack, but after hearing what I just heard I had lost my appetite. I didn't know how I was going to tell Kymani and Cyn was the first person I thought about calling. As I was driving, I felt like someone was following me and for a minute I thought I saw Talia and Tevin driving behind me, but shrugged it off because why the two of them would be together. I guess I was just being paranoid after what I had just heard on that tape.

"What the fuccckkkkkk?" I saw the car speeding at me but there was nowhere for me to go. I tried to brace myself as the driver seemed to have lost control of the wheel and rammed right into me.

BOOM! The impact of the crash had me feeling dazed and just when I thought it was all over the driver backed up and rammed into me again. Everything seemed fuzzy as I heard Cyn screaming in the background, but I couldn't get the words out that I was trapped in my seat. *Lord, please take care of Kymani and Azia and make sure that Cyn is good. Everything I've ever done I hope you know there was a reason for it all.* I prayed before everything went black and I lost consciousness.

TO BE CONTINUED...

Interested in becoming a part of the Treasured Publications family?

Submit manuscripts to
Info@Treasuredpub.com
Like us on Facebook:
Treasured Publications

Be sure to text **Treasured** to **22828**
To subscribe to our Mailing List.
Never miss a release or contest again!

CPSIA information can be obtained
at www.ICGtesting.com
Printed in the USA
LVOW13s1545160217
524503LV00009B/636/P

9 781542 934930